TOO LATE

Denise Wright Lund

BOOKSIDE Press

Copyright © 2024 by Denise Wright Lund

ISBN: 978-1-77883-525-4 (Paperback)

All rights reserved. No part of this publication may be reproduced, distributed, or transmitted in any form or by any means, including photocopying, recording, or other electronic or mechanical methods, without the prior written permission of the publisher, except in the case brief quotations embodied in critical reviews and other noncommercial uses permitted by copyright law.

The views expressed in this book are solely those of the author and do not necessarily reflect the views of the publisher, and the publisher hereby disclaims any responsibility for them.

BOOKSIDE Press

BookSide Press
877-741-8091
www.booksidepress.com
orders@booksidepress.com

Dedication

To My Wonderful Daddy God
{You believed in me}
His Beloved Son My Lord And
Savior Jesus Christ,
My Compassionate Best Friend The Holy Spirit,
Thank You For Your Presence!!!
God The Father
God The Son
God The Holy Spirit
This book is only possible because of you!!!
More of you my awesome Daddy God, less of me!!!

Contents

Acknowledgments	**vii**
Foreword	**ix**
Introduction	**xi**
Part 1 - Life is precious on Earth	**1**
Chapter 1: Who Died	3
Chapter 2: Looking Back	27
Chapter 3: They Meet	48
Part 2 - Life is Forgotten in Hell	**71**
Chapter 4: Final Days	72
Chapter 5: No Return	92
Chapter 6: Out of Grace	117
About the Author	**149**
Bibliography	**155**

Acknowledgments

1. My wonderful husband, he never stopped believing in me and encouraging me. You are my best friend, my soul-mate and lover. I will always thank God for you Mark Lund. Thank you for helping me with the completion of this book my righteous husband.

2. My wonderful children and grandchildren. You are my inspiration and joy! Thank you for believing in me and for all of your prayers. Thank you for loving God. My greatest achievement is knowing we will all be together in Heaven. That is success to me!

3. Sarah Lemley who attended Indian River Charter High School created the book cover.

4. My dear friend Teresa Gangloff who edited this book. Amy Snyder my niece created inside pictures. Amy Snyder, Brittany Rank, Sydney & Ashleigh Lovell, Gene & Marcia Barkan also contributed their computer skills. Alison LoBasso burned inspirational CDs for me to listen to while I worked.

5. Three incredible and powerful men of God who were more than just Pastor, Preacher and Teacher to me, they became personal friends, I'll always have such admiration and respect for each of you! Thank you, Billy Mikler, Gary Montecalvo and Paul Hall!

6. Christian radio stations 91.9 Christian FM. Vero Beach, Florida, Positive Z88.3 Orlando, Florida. I absolutely love them. Hours upon hours of studying God's word, I would listen to Christian radio to keep my complete focus on listening to the Holy Spirit, while writing this book. Thank you, you are awesome!

7. Mel Gibson I have to applaud you, you made the greatest movie I have ever seen. The Passion of the Christ! You are an incredible Actor, Writer and Director. Thank You!

Foreword

Satan and the fallen angels are working hard to deceive the world. Satan has his command set up in the heavenly realm, also known as the second heaven and sends many demons to earth to lead Gods children astray.

After many tears for our young and lost generation, the Holy Spirit revealed to me to write this book. I am just a messenger, sharing an important life changing and much needed message. I know Gods anointing is on this book and the Holy Spirit will minister to everyone that reads this powerful book.

Be afraid; be very afraid, time is running out! Make sure you are ready before it is Too Late for you!

Warning!!! This book will change your life and save your soul.

Introduction

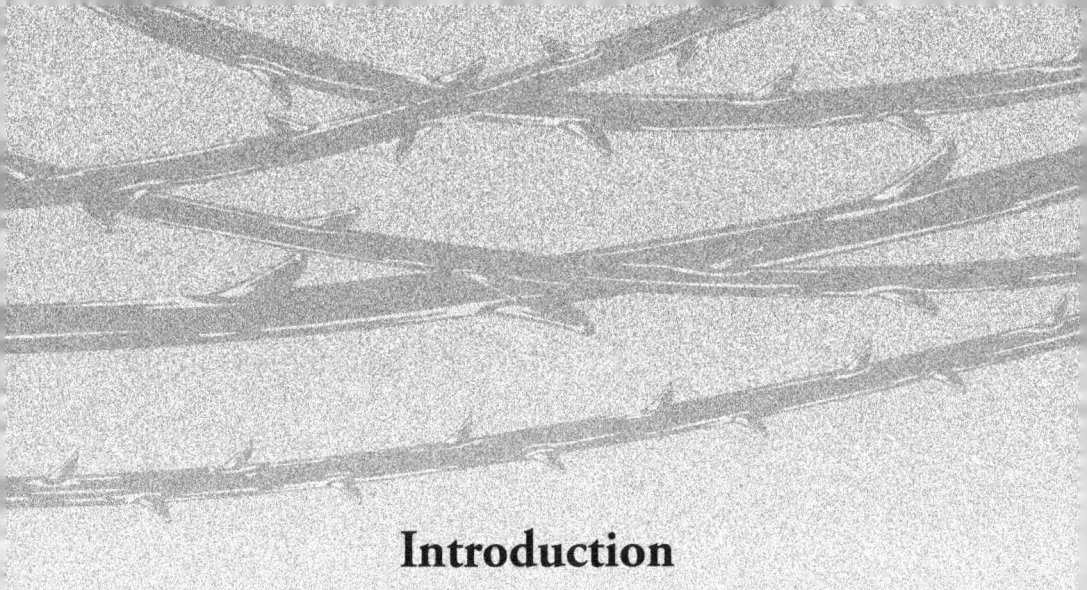

While reading the daily newspaper, again I was sickened. Four boys, between the ages of 13 and 15 years old, splashed a 15-year-old boy with rubbing alcohol and ignited it, causing burns over two-thirds of his young body. How horrifying, this is only one of the many shocking stories about our young, disobedient, lost generation.

Last year at a high school not far from where I live, again something horrible happened. A sports game was played; the game was lost. While on the way home from the game, a few of the boys in the back of the bus placed the blame of their lost game to one young man. They pinned him down in the back of the bus, pulled down his pants and sodomized him with an object.

A 63-year-old man and father of four, was working in his back yard, when five young men between the ages of 20 and 23, attacked him from behind they hit his head with a cinder block. He died in the hospital. The attackers ransacked his home and took a television, some cash and cell phones.

My husband and I witnessed two cars full of teenagers racing and hit an innocent man. To our surprise, my husband knew the man that was hit and killed. Sadly, he also knew his now widowed wife and fatherless precious little girl.

The suicide rate has sadly escalated. I had a friend whose son hung himself and I have another friend [whose voice I still hear on a saved voice mail] who shot and killed himself.

There are so many adults and teenagers that do drugs. One boy who called me mom overdosed on drugs and became brain-dead. I could not stop crying, I felt like I had failed him. His family had to make an awful decision and pull the plug.

The horrible stories go on and on! This book addresses parents and teen-agers, and reveals to them there will be consequences for their sins! I pray it will literally scare the Hell out of anyone who reads it and they obediently turn back to God!

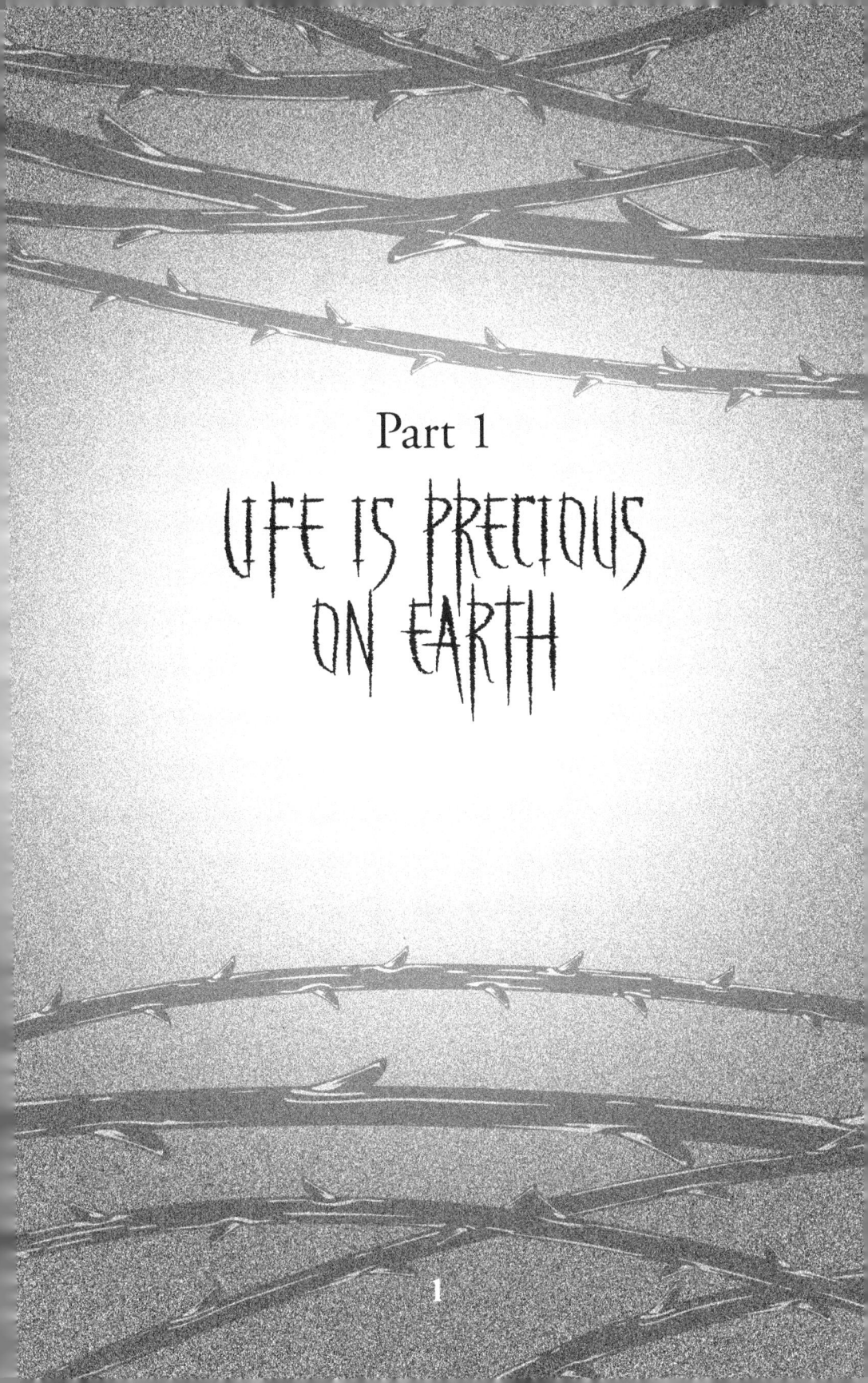

Part 1
LIFE IS PRECIOUS ON EARTH

Chapter 1
WHO DIED

As you read this book you will need to understand three important points.

The first point is there is a main story of typical everyday kids who made detrimental choices while alive on this earth; their choices cost them dearly.

The second important point is, I will narrate off from the main story while using Biblical scriptures to prove important points you need to remember.

The third important point is Earth is real, Heaven and so is Hell. Please take this story seriously.

Bible stands for {**B**asic **I**nstructions **B**efore **L**eaving **E**arth}. Do not wait before its {**Too Late**} for you! Life is precious on Earth! Life is forgotten in Hell! Let us begin our powerful story.

Five dear friends that hung out together all the time have just yelled Happy New Year. This was their justified reason to drink, be crazy and wild. They had allowed alcohol to control them. How sad, an automobile accident took the lives of all five of these typical reckless young kids. The ages of these five young adults that unrepentedly passed away were between sixteen and eighteen years old. Some people would consider this age still inexperienced children.

Only one of the kids that died returned back into his lifeless body on earth, to tell his horrific story about the afterlife experience. The other four had the misfortune of feeling life itself prematurely snatched from their God given young bodies on earth and experience the last breath of air being taken from them. They were not able to return to their bodies on earth, these kids were not given a second chance.

[We cannot possibly imagine or fathom this because we are still very much alive on this earth. But one day soon we will all experience death and we had better be ready. It is coming for you!]

{Luke 12:5 …But I'll tell you whom to fear, Fear God, who has the power to kill you and then throw you into hell. Yes, he's the one to fear.}

[Be Afraid, Be Very Afraid]

Though they died here on this earth, as we know death, they are still very, very much alive, and this life is forever and ever, another thing we really do not comprehend. Let's look at where these kids are now living due to their poor choices while alive on earth. There is definitely life after death.

Twenty-two years have passed since the devastating accident occurred. Life still goes on and the only people to even think of these poor unfortunate kids are family members who may have a previous photo of their child to look upon. These family members still have their lives to complete here on this unpredictable earth. Everyone else they knew in school or grew up with never even thinks of these four teenagers. Who were these kids and where are they now living?

PAIGE

One of the four teenagers that died was a young beautiful brunette at age seventeen named Paige. You would have thought she had her whole life to conquer. Paige was raised by her mother; a very mystical woman named Holly whose source of income was psychic and palm readings. Holly also fostered kids for extra income. Holly had become Paige's world; it was the two of them against everyone else. Paige never knew her dad, he split when she was just a baby.

Paige was never brought to church and never taught about our heavenly God the awesome Father, His Son Jesus Christ who came to this earth and died so that we could be forgiven and have eternity in heaven above, and the wonderful Holy Spirit who stays and comforts our every need.

[This is important parents; give your child a spiritual foundation!!!]

{Proverbs 22:6 … Train up your child in the way he should go, and when he is old, he will not depart from it.}

[Be Afraid, Be Very Afraid]

Paige was taught the complete opposite. At the young age of thirteen, she lost her virginity to a man in his twenties, who was one of her mother's clients for psychic readings. Paige's upbringing without a father figure twisted her view on men. She learned how to get attention as her young breast developed and her body matured.

For Paige's sixteenth birthday, her mother bought her a crystal to perform her own psychic readings. Paige loved her crystal and with it tied to a string, she would ask it many questions. If the crystal swung to each side back and forth that was a no or if it swung the opposite way in front of her that was a yes. The crystal was what she turned to for answers.

The mystical [deceiving] crystal was all she needed to get her answers. Paige never talked to God and when some friends tried to share the truth about Jesus Christ Gods Son our wonderful and compassionate Savior, she shut them up quickly and shared about her crystal. Paige loved anything to do with the dark of night. She loved scary horror movies. Halloween was her favorite holiday, if it was spooky or creepy she loved it.

Paige never really thought about death. She believed when you died you were reincarnated or you became a ghost. Paige did not believe in God or Satan. Paige wishes, she would have known the truth while she was alive on this earth before it was {**Too Late**} for her. Many years have passed since the accident.

[Where was Paige brought after she died? Well let's just say she is still on Earth.]

{Ezekiel 31:17… yet you shall be brought down… to the depths of the earth.}

[Be Afraid, Be Very Afraid]

The place where Paige has been living is an unimaginable and indescribable horror, absolutely horrid!!! Later on in this story we will view the absolute terror of how each teenager reached their final destination. But for now, we are going to visit each one of these hopelessly lost teenagers one by one and see where they are living forever because of their wrong choices while alive on earth.

[Remember they have been here for at least twenty-two years! They are lost and doomed; no one can help them, no one! Life on earth is so short so very, very short, like water that quickly evaporates in the air, it appears and in an instant, disappears.]

{James 4:14… why, you do not even know what will happen tomorrow. What is your life? You are a mist that appears for a little while and then vanishes.}

[Be Afraid, Be Very Afraid]

Deep down to the center of the earth, yes, it has been proven full of lava and unbearable heat, a heat that with an earthly form would be consumed in seconds. But this is no longer your earthly body.

[Jesus returned after death and shared I am flesh and bones touch me. You will have a new body, your eternal body with all your senses, you smell, you see, you hear, you taste, and yes you feel! You will be alive with flesh and bones!]

{Luke 24:39… they were still talking about this, Jesus himself stood among them and said to them, "Why are you troubled, and why do doubts rise in your minds? Look at my hands and feet. It is I myself! Touch me and see; a ghost does not have flesh and bones, as you see I have."}

[Be Afraid, Be Very Afraid]

Hell has different levels of torture and torment. Satan is lord here and thrives on it. All who dwell in this sad and forgotten place must call Satan lord. You will be brought before the master of lies and deception who is Satan, and he will choose your final destination in hell.

Paige was placed in the black dungeon cell; there are far worse tormented areas but all are horrendous. Paige was brought here because of her life on earth, she aided in deceiving others to believing in the powers of the crystal and darkness and to sin. This helped Satan gather more captives for eternal torture, everlasting pain and suffering and away from the truth and fellowship with God.

[Don't fool yourself; if you are not walking with peace and fellowship with God and know His awesome presence, then you may be heading for everlasting destruction.]

{2 Thessalonians 1:9… they will be punished with eternal destruction and shut out from the presence of the Lord and from the Majesty of his power…}

[Be Afraid, Be Very Afraid]

Paige's cries are not as strong as they were when she first came here, but the moaning and whimpering never stops; only when the demons come to add excruciating pain to Paige do her screams increase. There are no tears for her cries, no liquid of any kind in hell, just pure excruciating, tormenting pain and screams.

The blackness of hell can be felt. You cannot describe it. You will never see the sunshine again, not even a flicker of a star. What God intended as a blessing, two eyes to see with, here in hell only adds more terror?

As the fire comes closer to Paige's cell, the continued fire that forever and ever sweeps through hell on and on and on. The fire surrounds the walls and the cell is lit up, sadly, now we can see inside the cell because of this flesh and bone burning, unquenchable fire.

There is Paige curled up in a fetal position, she is covered in worms, they crawl all through her. She knows the fire is coming for her. She is crying with what little strength she has. Paige still has her mind, this adds to so many regrets and the missing of her mom Holly. Paige knows it's only just a matter of time when her deceived and misguided mother will one day also be captive and be forever and ever tortured by Satan.

If only her mom can find out about the truth of God and not come to this horrible place before it is {**Too Late**}. Paige continues to cry out, the insufferable, unbearable flames soon would add to more torture.

The worms have been eating at her all these years, she feels every one of them continually crawling on and through her, they will not die like her, and the fire is never quenched. The only light in this God forsaken place hurts so bad, so unimaginably bad.

[Don't Rebel against God!]

{Isaiah 66:24… and they will go out and look upon the dead bodies of those who rebelled against God; their worm will not die, nor will their fire be quenched…}

[Be Afraid, Be Very Afraid]

Paige's hearing has also become forever anguish, her ears are burned off to the bone and sadly, she is surrounded by all the multitudes of lost and hopeless people, who like herself are continually tortured and continually screaming in agony.

This life is for all people who chose sin and Satan, over purity and God. We have so little time here on earth. This is so sad, millions, upon millions of people, wishing they had made a different choice while alive on earth.

The flames are coming upon her, and Paige rises to her skeleton knees to once again endure the unbelievable, unimaginable pain. Her flesh has been burned off to the bone in many areas, remember this is your forever body, everything will be much slower, and you will feel it all intensely!!! Her mouth opens wide while screaming and suffering in pain, this is also difficult because her mouth has no water, and it's completely dry.

She looks like someone who had been set on fire for committing witchcraft in the olden days on earth. Try to imagine that going on and on and on. You would think the fire was alive the way it crept in to the cell to consume its prey. And inside the cell is a seventeen-year-old girl named Paige. Paige is absolutely pitiful to look upon; to imagine one day she ate and drank whatever she wished, enjoyed the beach, watched movies with her mother, and fornicated with Alex her boyfriend. This is so pitiful and so very, very real and sad.

Paige has no hair, just a couple of strands hanging on the back of her scorched, burned, bald skeleton head. One of her eyes has been burned completely out. She has no nose it has been burned off, but she is still able to smell. Another one of our God given senses that was meant for good only now will be used to torment her.

[Demons are disgusting to look upon and so foul to smell!]

{Revelation 18:2… a prison for every foul and unclean spirit.}

[Be Afraid, Be Very Afraid]

The smell in hell is so bad you will want to vomit! It is absolutely disgusting, foul, and rotten beyond belief. When you drive by a dead animal that has laid dead awhile, maggots will form and the stench is so intolerable you can't stand it, this is nothing. A rotten egg by itself has turned my stomach, times that by a thousand.

Hell is pure rotted, disgusting, foul evil!

Hell is millions, upon millions, upon millions of people who are lost, and will be forever tormented and tortured, the smell is the smell of all of these people whose very flesh falls around them and rots.

As Paige feels around when the fire briefly leaves her pitiful skeleton frame of a body, she feels the maggots that have come from her very own body's fallen rotted flesh. Like I said, no one can help her, and she knows this. This is where she will remain throughout all eternity.

The cell floor and walls are made of stone, [no soft beds for full night's sleep here] and she will never sleep again. The size of her cell is no bigger than a table that seats four people. Try to imagine how that would be as a permanent eternal residence.

Back to Paige's cries and whimpers only to hear the millions, upon millions who join in the cries of horror and torment in hell. Paige has no lips but you see teeth, most of her body is burned of ash, just a pitiful skeleton frame with hanging flesh.

TOO LATE

[Remember this scripture please and save yourself from this hopelessness!]

{Hebrews 13:20-21 ... Dear Lord, may you, the God of peace, who brought again from the dead our Lord Jesus; equip us with all we need for doing your will. Please work in us what is pleasing to You, through the power of Jesus Christ, that great Shepherd of the sheep to whom be glory forever and ever, Amen.}

[Be Afraid, Be Very Afraid]

ALEX

Alex was another of the unfortunate kids that lost his life in the accident that early New Years Day. Alex is the oldest of the teenagers; still he was only eighteen when he died. Alex was also Paige's boyfriend at the time, which will only add to extra torment as you further read.

Born to Frank and Peggy Stark, Alex was born into money and luxury; he was an only child. His father did very well as a life insurance agent; he eventually ran the Merritt Island office. Alex was always given the very best of everything. By the age of three, he already had mini motorcycles and a mini jeep, his dad spoiled him.

[He was never taught to share, or to give of one's self in anything, it's all about me was how he was raised.]

{Matthew 16:24-26... Then Jesus said to his disciples, "If anyone would come after me, he must deny himself and take up his cross and follow me. For whoever wants to save his life will lose it, but whoever loses his life for me will find it. What good will it be for man if he gains the whole world, yet forfeits his soul to Hell?"}

[Be Afraid, Be Very Afraid]

Alex never knew hunger or poverty. He was always handed money by both parents, and he knew how to manipulate his parents to benefit himself further. Alex never noticed any homeless individuals hoping for some change to eat with.

One particular incident occurred with a pathetic homeless gentleman and Alex; it was meant to change Alex's path but sadly didn't. On Alex's sixteenth birthday his father bought him a red sports Thunderbird car. Alex was in love with the car, almost as much as he loved himself. Alex knew he looked good in it. He would be the envy of everyone, and that pleased him.

One day, while he was out driving, he drove up to the store jumped out of his car and walked by an elderly man. This man looked homeless, definitely poor, his clothing was rags and his shoes were duck taped together, one of his feet was partly cut off. The poor gentleman looked deep in Alex's eyes as Alex passed by him; he needed some money for food or something to drink. Alex didn't even look at the poor unfortunate man. Alex was above this pathetic person's class, so Alex assumed. Alex had hundreds in his wallet; money mommy and daddy provided him with freely.

One of Alex's rules that he gave himself was, never keep pennies, he was above that so on his way out of the store, Alex made a comment as he walked by the gentleman and threw the three pennies down in front of him, "Here have some cents get a job." Alex was so arrogant and full of himself.

You would almost think the pitiful elderly man was trying to reach out and touch Alex's self-centered heart. When Alex jumped in his car, he looked one last time at the man in rags. To Alex's amazement, the man was gone, he had disappeared! Alex looked bewildered but didn't think much of this; he was too consumed with his new sports car.

[Don't underestimate God's love for you. He knows our hearts and wants us to spend eternity with Him in His almighty kingdom. However, we are still in control of our own will.]

Alex is selfish and self-centered. The man he just walked by was an angel sent by God. The angel was attempting to teach Alex to have a heart for others and give of one's self. This was one of the many times God had reached out to have a personal relationship with Alex and save him from despair.

{Exodus 23:20… The Lord said, "I am sending an angel ahead of you to guard you along the way and bring you to the place I have prepared."}

[Be Afraid, Be Very Afraid]

Alex's parents went to church when they were younger, but as they got older, they had made few attempts to go. They only go once a year on Easter Sunday. Alex doesn't even do that.

He was never taught the importance of having a personal relationship with God. Alex believes you have to do something awful like rape or murder to go to Hell that only the very bad people go there, like Hitler or Bundy.

[Again, don't let Satan deceive you; a lie can keep you from fellowship with God, which will keep you out of Heaven!]

{Revelation 21:8 … and all liars- their place will be in the fiery lake of burning sulfur. Hell!}

[Be Afraid, Be Very Afraid]

Alex's parents drifted apart while Alex was in his early teens. His mother realized his father's late-night appointments were taking way too long. She followed him a few nights where she discovered his favorite hangout was a Cocoa beach topless bar, The Sinner Room. When she investigated further, she also found out he had several women on the side he would visit.

They remained married but slept in separate bedrooms on either side of the house. This did not really upset Alex, not while he was so spoiled with life. Lots of money and the control of having everything nice was his only drive in life.

Alex was very self-centered, arrogant and full of pride. At the age of seventeen he started selling drugs for even more money. He had it all, a beautiful girlfriend, lots and lots of money, and drugs. He didn't have to work very hard for any of it. Alex was nominated the most likely to succeed in high school. Alex was on top of the world, he had the best of everything. Life was only going to get better and go on and on and on, so he thought.

How sad, if only his parents had turned to God in a more personal way, once a year would keep any friendship apart and Easter was not enough personal time with God. How sad, God wants a personal relationship with us, we are His children and He loves us so much; God knows the final outcome.

God did not make Hell for any of us, this horrible place was made for Satan and his fallen angels but our own will being self-driven, prideful, unforgiving and greed will bring us there.

[**Who is Satan?** In Revelation 12:7-12… You understand that Satan and one-third of the provoked angels fought for control in Heaven and lost the battle. He was hurled to the earth, and his angels with him. He is filled with fury.]

[Satan always attacks God's people. Much more happened at Christ's birth, death, and resurrection than most people realize. A war between the forces of good and evil was under way. With Christ's resurrection, Satan's ultimate defeat was assured. Originally Satan was an angel of God, but through his own pride, he became corrupt. The devil is God's enemy. Even though the devil is very powerful, as we can see by the condition of our world, he is always under God's control. He was once the greatest of all spirits that ministered unto our Lord. We see from the word of God that Satan allowed "pride" and "self" to cause his fall, leading to rebellion against God Almighty. Satan's eternal destination will be Hell for all eternity! Remain true and obedient to God, you will be protected, have eternal life with God not eternal death with Satan.]

So like Satan, Alex was full of pride and self. Satan enjoyed breaking and torturing Alex, he wasn't so tough anymore. To look upon Alex now is so sad and pathetic, absolutely pitiful. Alex was placed in the pits.

Remember it is black, black, and black beyond belief. The unquenchable fire is hungry for his bones and what little flesh is still on him and this fire is creeping towards him. Imagine a fire pit with logs when you start the fire it attaches itself to the logs, Alex is the log in the pit.

Imagine what the fire pit is like when it goes out, it is left with dusty soot, ashes and smothering smoke that is one of the reasons for wailing and gnashing of teeth. He can't breathe and the unbelievable smoke coming out of the pit is from Alex's own agonizing body because again he was the log that was on fire.

{Matthew 13:42 … there will be wailing and gnashing of teeth.}

[Be Afraid, Be Very Afraid]

Alex cannot get a full breath. Alex is gasping and gasping to breathe, only to breathe in smoke forever and ever.

[Imagine a fish out of water, gasping for air, this is nothing compared to what Alex is going through; the fish will eventually, die. Alex will not be so lucky.]

He is sitting with his hands around his skeleton knees. Like Paige, underneath Alex's skeleton frame, he can feel the maggots from his own rotted flesh, and the worms are a never-ending anguish. You will never rest, or be granted any peace.

{Isaiah 14:11… the maggot is spread under you and the worms will cover you.}

[Be Afraid, Be Very Afraid]

The worms are enjoying tormenting Alex; they help in removing his flesh and will crawl through him continually.

His permanent place of forever torture and unbearable pain is this pit. It's the size of a fireplace; imagine someone forever being burned alive in it, and Satan constantly striking a match to lavish in your [forever-unbearable torture.] Imagine this small area it is so sad and so very real.

Alex has less flesh than Paige on his pitiful skeletal frame. Every time Alex would crawl out of this awful pit trying to escape, because he could not bear any more pain and suffering, a grotesque and disgusting, huge demon would ascend from nowhere and tear at Alex's flesh, and throw him back into this unbearable hole.

To look at Alex would make you cry, this was a good-looking athletic kid. His favorite sports were football and surfing. Alex will never play or watch football or feel the breathtaking, refreshing ocean on his body, ever, ever again. Alex will never feel love, or fornicate with anyone ever again. He has no hope, and will be forever lost, and forgotten, and he knows and feels it all.

His mind is there; his cries are joined with the many others who sadly made wrong choices while alive on earth. Satan is a liar, and will attempt to make anything look appealing to keep you.

[Satan wants to hurt God, and it hurts God to lose fellowship and eternity with us, we are his precious children. God is always there to help, providing refuge, security, and peace. God's power is complete and his ultimate victory is certain. He will not fail to rescue those who love him. God is all the strength we need.]

{Psalm 46:1… God is our refuge and strength, an ever-present help in trouble.}

[Be Afraid, Be Very Afraid]

[There are so many Alex's in our world today, full of pride and self; it's the all about me person that thinks they are all that, they are about material things, and money, that's their success. They judge everyone's success by their wealth, and what they own.

I would rather be there for others, be dirt poor, humble, appreciative and spend eternity in heaven, than only think of myself, be prideful, greedy, and wealthy with so much money one cannot fathom and spend eternity in hell. **Hello!!!**]

[It is very difficult to have a personal relationship with God when you are a proud person and not humble.]

{Proverbs 16:19 … It is better to be of a humble spirit with the poor and lowly, than to divide the wealth with the proud.}

[Be Afraid, Be Very Afraid]

For now we will leave Alex's charred, burnt, pitiful skeleton frame with hanging flesh, and sadly visit the third child that died.

Lucky

Lucky's real name was Lector; he was nicknamed Lucky by one of his foster parents. Born to a heroin addict, this poor little African American baby was underfed and left in soiled diapers. From the moment of birth, this little guy fought to survive. By the time he was discovered, he was near dead and rushed to the hospital, he had to go through drug withdrawals as a tiny newborn.

The state took Lucky to a foster family who had three other foster boys they were caring for. This was a warm and loving family. His foster mother nicknamed him Lucky, because he was still alive. The boys would call her Meme. When Lucky was five Meme was diagnosed with breast cancer; she could no longer be able to care for the boys.

It was a very sad day when the state came to take the boys to other foster homes. Lucky could not stop crying, this was the only mother he had ever known and he loved her very much. The boys were separated, the two youngest stayed together that was Lucky and Kevin; Kevin was two years older. They were happy to at least have each other. The next foster home they went to was not so pleasant. Miss Kate was African American; she was strict and abusive, they had to call her Miss Kate. She called them little Negro troubled boys.

When she would leave to go to the store she would tie them to a chair. One time Lucky could not hold his bladder while being tied up, he urinated on himself and on her chair. When Miss Kate returned, she beat him all over with a ruler.

Lucky began hating women at a young age because of this abusive, uncompassionate woman. When Lucky was nine and tied to a chair, he managed to get his wrists free, leaving rope burn marks embedded deep in his flesh. When Miss Kate returned, she beat him with the ruler across the face and head. The corner of the ruler cut a gash next to his eye that required stitches.

The hospital reported Miss Kate and once again the boys were taken away. Lucky sadly was with Miss Kate for four years. It was so sad for Lucky, the only brother he knew was Kevin and he was to be taken to a different home than Lucky. Now he had no family left to speak of.

The family Lucky was brought to was the first Caucasian family he had experienced. The husband was a truck driver and gone a lot. The wife cared for another boy who was also Caucasian and a few years older than Lucky. They became close friends. The boys had to attend church every Sunday; this was where God tried to reach out to Lucky many times. Lucky might not have had anyone who totally loved him, but God did, and wanted Lucky to know and feel His wonderful presence.

Timmy was the other foster boy Lucky had become close to. A lot of times they would skip church together; their foster mom, Mama Stella never even knew they were skipping. When Lucky was only thirteen, Timmy was fifteen and felt he was drawn to boys more than girls; Timmy began fondling Lucky, this was causing stimulation for both boys. Lucky felt he didn't like girls either, because of Miss Kate. This went on for a year, and Lucky lost his innocence to another boy.

{Romans 1:26-27… *Because of this, God gave them over to shameful lusts. Even their women exchanged natural relations for unnatural ones. In the same way the men also abandoned natural relations with women and were inflamed with lust for one another. Men committed indecent acts with other men, and received in themselves the due penalty for perversion.*}

[Be Afraid, Be Very Afraid]

When Mama Stella busted the boys in their sexual acts, she had Lucky taken again to another foster home. Lucky had been going to church for five years with this foster family; God tried so hard to have a personal relationship with Lucky.

Lucky was fourteen and taken to Holly's house; this is where he met Paige and they became close. They would introduce themselves as brother and sister; this was amusing to them because he was African American and she was Caucasian. Even though Lucky was in the tenth grade now and Paige was in the eleventh grade, Paige let Lucky hang out with her everywhere she went.

Lucky became good friends with Alex, Paige's boyfriend, and the three of them are in the depths of Hell, together forever! Lucky cared deeply for Paige and Holly, they were good to him but what they instilled in Lucky was far from the truth about God, His Son Jesus Christ and the Holy Spirit.

Lucky learned about tarot card readings, which was his favorite where Paige's favorite was the crystal. Lucky didn't really have a strong belief in anything, he believed when you die that was it; you just get buried in the ground there is no life after death.

Lucky was sixteen years old when the automobile accident took his young life. This is so very sad. Where will Lucky spend eternity? Satan cast Lucky into the lake of fire where many homosexuals were cast.

The lake of fire and brimstone is well over a mile long and the only place in hell that is always lit up. There are people everywhere in the lake of fire, all in excruciating pain, screaming and whaling.

The only thing Lucky has not yet experienced is the worms and demons eating at his flesh. He already experienced demons tearing him apart, and ripping flesh from his bones, in Satan's dungeon. We cannot imagine what this poor child is experiencing nor do we want to; his skin continually burning by lava and fire. Hell is very real and Lucky knows this to be true.

It is {**Too Late**} for Lucky. Lucky has been in burning lava and fire for years.

The first part of his stay in hell was in the dungeon of horror with Satan. Remember there is no rest day or night, that means every second, of every minute, of every hour, of every day, of every month, of every year, he feels unbearable pain and suffering.

When Lucky was in the accident that took his life on earth, part of his hand was cut off. When you go to hell if you had a missing limb, it still will be gone. God restores your body, you will be rewarded in Heaven, and you will have eternal happiness and peace. The opposite occurs in hell, Lucky's partly cut off hand is down to pure skeletal remains.

[The lake has many lost people, all crying out in unimaginable torture, forever and ever!]

{Revelation 20:10… was cast into the lake of fire and brimstone and they will be tormented day and night forever and ever.}

[Be Afraid, Be Very Afraid]

When the demon tossed Lucky in the lake of fire, he had already spent many years as Satan's personal captive. There was really no flesh left on him. The fiery lake of ash and lava has devoured the rest away. He is just a burned skeleton now; there is a misty grayish form you see inside the skeleton. Lucky keeps reaching his hands up and screaming with what little strength he has, it is mainly just pitiful moans now. His soul is trapped in his own skeleton frame and he will never die.

Lucky only had sixteen years alive on this earth; he did not deserve to be forever tortured like this, no one does.

[This was not Gods choosing, we are turned over to make our own choices while alive on earth. Please don't let Satan deceive you, he only wishes to hurt God and by taking your eternal destiny from fellowship with God; Satan won. No matter what you are dealing with remain faithful and true to God. Satan is out of the presence of the Lord. He wants you out of God's wonderful presence also.]

{Job 2:7 … so Satan went out from the presence of the Lord.…}

[Be Afraid, Be Very Afraid]

Jayden

There are many levels of torment in hell, Jayden is the saddest that I will write about. Jayden is the fourth child that died at the accident!

Jayden was born into a very religious and strict family. Her father Will, a preacher, would have Sunday church service at their house... That was fine; however, his controlling, self-righteous and judging personality did not allow Jayden to even praise God in any other churches. Jayden rebelled. Jayden was so beautiful and full of life growing up, with her fun optimistic personality, she even brought several friends to their Sunday service at her house, and they asked Jesus to be Lord of their lives.

Jayden was so precious to God, and at age eight, she asked the Lord Jesus into her heart. Some of her saved friends found other churches with youth groups to attend. They would invite her many times to come with them and meet other young kids like herself that worshiped and praised God.

Jayden wanted so badly to attend, but as a young obedient child she would honor her parents' wishes and not go. Her father and mother had many reasons for never allowing her to attend other churches.

Her mother Judy taught her a saying that went something like this, "faults in others I can see, praise the Lord there's none in me."

Will found out the kids who went to other churches would invite Jayden to attend and would raise their hands in praise; he was against this type of worship. The controlling strictness from her parents angered Jayden; this was the only tool Satan needed to get Jayden away from the presence of God.

One incident that hurt Jayden the most was when her parents would not allow her to go with her friends to a revival for young kids called Acquire the Fire, Jayden never got over it. Her father and mothers self-righteous, judging and controlling ways, eventually is what contributed to ending Jayden's personal relationship with her Daddy God.

{Matthew 7:1 … "Do not judge, or you too will be judged."}

[Be Afraid, Be Very Afraid]

   Jayden would respect her parents' wishes while she was young, but as she became a teenager she began to rebel. She was always her father's favorite, and she would also be her father's heartbreak.

   Jayden had three older siblings, a brother and two sisters. Her father sold vacuum cleaners and had his own shop. Judy her mother was a homemaker. Jayden really didn't know Eve, her older sister of twelve years very well. Jayden's brother who was ten years older than her was her favorite, his name was Matthew. Matthew was always very fun and loving to her. The sister that was four years older named Nelly was most annoying and Jayden was not close to her at all. She always had to be the center of attention and it didn't matter who she hurt.

   If her parents could see Jayden now, they would have done things different. Control is what they thought of first, and they used different scriptures in the Bible to manipulate, control and justify their twisted un-Christ like actions.

[Jayden's parents should have understood and accepted their daughter's wish to visit youth groups that believed in our Holy God and his precious Son Jesus Christ.]

{Philippians 2:4-5 … Each of you should look not only to your own interests, but also to the interests of others. Your attitude should be the same as that of Christ Jesus.}

[Be Afraid, Be Very Afraid]

[Satan really wanted Jayden; it is better to have never known God then to have known Him and turned away from Him.]

One of the kids that Jayden brought home to their church service got saved; he ended up becoming a youth leader. This young man was used as an instrument in the salvation of a lot of people. Satan blamed Jayden for that and focused on her rebellion and anger towards her parents to get her away from fellowship with God. Satan caused her anger to grow and grow until one day she refused to even pray.

This hurt God so much, His beloved daughter that use to always talk to Him, now would not communicate with Him; Satan loved hurting God with one of His precious children.

Jayden knew by not praying to God this would hurt her parents and why not hurt them, they hurt her. One thing that also bothered her parents was the fact that Paige had become Jayden's best friend and Paige did not believe in God at all.

They had become best friends in tenth grade and were in eleventh grade when the car crash took their young lives.

Neither Paige, Alex, Lucky nor even Jayden think of each other, yet they are all here in hell together. Sadly, while alive on earth they use to joke and say well if we go to hell all of our friends will be there.

[You can't joke about Hell, it is a very real place with a lot of people who will experience so much pain and suffering for the rest of eternity.]

When Jayden was a young girl, she got trapped in a small rest room; because of this she became very claustrophobic. Jayden could not even ride elevators; she had become absolutely terrified of small areas. Her palms would sweat, her heart would beat so very fast even at the thought of a closed in area. This phobia was absolutely terrifying for her. This beautiful, precious, positive child will spend eternity living her greatest fear.

Satan will hurt you. He knows everything about you, and will use what he can to deceive you. He is the complete opposite of God, Satan is beyond description evil. He relishes in the fact that Jayden had walked away from her eternal right to walk in perfect harmony, beauty, eternal peace and happiness with Jesus.

Satan loved the fact that Jayden had been so precious and close to God, he knew this would hurt God his arch-enemy. Jayden was Satan's and he could do with her as he wished. Satan loathed and detested Jayden and she was going to suffer greatly forever and ever.

Later on in the book you will see how very sad it was when Jayden was turned over to Satan. This child who turned her life over to Jesus at age eight, and helped bring several people into a personal relationship with our awesome Lord now belongs to Satan. Sadly, let's see where Jayden was placed for all eternity. Like I said, Jayden is in an absolutely horrific place; hell is so bad and so very real.

This is where Satan sent Jayden. This area the demons work continually to add extra excruciating pain, and suffering. Satan is lord over all in hell. There are so many lost people here who at one time served God; all are screaming out and forever being tortured, this is indescribable.

Where is precious Jayden? You see demons adding extra pain to lost souls, and loving it. That is what they are doing to Jayden. There is so much sorrow here, how sad Jayden really did not seem wicked, but if you are not in fellowship with God, you will end up in darkness.

[Please don't fall out of the grace of God, like Jayden did.]

{Galatians 5:4…you have fallen away from grace.}

[Be Afraid, Be Very Afraid]

Satan had the foul, most disgusting, disfigured demons throw Jayden in a coffin, and seal it shut. Not only was she placed where she has the absolute greatest fear, but she will be forever tortured. She is alert, and alive, and absolutely terrified. Her forever home is a coffin that demons continually set on fire; like a hog being turned and roasted the demons continue to turn her burning coffin. I can't even describe how sad and pathetic Jayden is.

To remember her on earth as the fun and happy girl that use to love walking the beach and looking for seashells and her first love was Devin. She has remained alive in a coffin now for twenty-two years. She still has eternity!

[Think about that!]

Her screams are so sad. Jayden is on fire and the worms that share her coffin eat the little flesh that's left on her. The coffin is high enough in the air so the unquenchable fire can continue to burn her; she gets no break. The foul demons take turns jabbing a spear into open holes in the coffin for even more added torture. Each jab of a spear adds to a heartbreaking cry from Jayden but delightful noise to her tormentors. Jayden is just a pitiful skeleton now; her misty grayish soul will be forever tormented and tortured.

This is so sad, what was her greatest fear {small areas} Satan has used against her and she will live in this coffin throughout all of eternity. The demons actually take shifts so they can continue to stab at her coffin and light it on fire. Jayden's fate is to be screaming and crying out in agonizing pain and unbearable suffering forever. This was ordered by Satan.

Jayden's boyfriend and first love was Devin, a seventeen- year-old boy who also died in the accident, but was given a second chance and returned to his body on earth. Devin was terrified by the whole experience that he escaped hell. Sadly, he knows in his heart his dear friends did not.

{Matthew 23:33 … How can ye escape the damnation of hell?}

[Be Afraid, Be Very Afraid]

[This next chapter you read goes back to the beginning of our story.]

Chapter 2
Looking Back

*D*evin Chaplin is now a grown man thirty-nine years old; he is thinking back when he was seventeen, about the ordeal of his dear friends and his beloved girlfriend Jayden. Devin is also thinking about the horrible accident that took his life, and the realization that he escaped hell; sadly, he knows in his heart his dear friends did not!

Devin is a man who carries revelation knowledge deep within his heart and soul. He sits at his desk in front of his window. You can see he is deep in thought. Still as handsome a man as he was in his youth, blue eyes and blonde hair that overpowers his grayish sideburns. The slightly worn lines of his aging face only looks more intensified, because of where his heart and mind are.

Devin almost did not live to tell about the absolute horror and terror he witnessed and is now remembering. Wearing a short sleeve dress shirt, you see his left hand slightly rubbing underneath the sleeve of his upper right arm. When Devin slowly removes his hand, you see four deep uneven scars with permanent blackish gray marks embedded into his flesh.

These scars looked as if they were deliberate, like something latched on, and burned deep into his skin. Obviously, these scars go hand in hand with what is weighing so heavy on Devin's heart.

Its morning now and looking outside the office window you see the radiant sunshine. Devin is trying to change his thoughts for some kind of peace of mind. The green from the trees and grass, the beautiful flowerbeds are beaming with kindness and love. This is all so breathtaking and beautiful.

"How could there be such great evil and complete horror that really does exist, while looking around at so much beauty?" Devin thought as he remembered his horrific ordeal.

{Revelation 17:8 … the beast that you saw will ascend out of the bottomless pit.}

[Be Afraid, Be Very Afraid]

As Devin stops staring outside the window, he looks over the top of his desk, to the right side is a worn black Bible. He slides the Bible in front of himself and begins to gently rub the top. Devin knew what was inside and hesitated for a few seconds. Still, with deep thought he opens the Bible, reaches inside and grabs a much familiar bookmarker. The bookmarker is an old four by six picture of five teenagers. Devin intensely grips the picture with both hands; his eyes begin to tear up while looking at it. There are three boys and two girls in the photo; Devin is the second boy from the right.

These were his dear friends from high school, the kids he hung out with, his companions and buddies. This is what has been so profound and full of meaning in Devin's heart and thoughts. Why wouldn't it be, just twenty-two years earlier at age seventeen Devin in an indescribable automobile accident?

All five of these unfortunate teenagers were in the car. The only one of the five kids to have escaped deaths profound grip was Devin. Devin's four friends, to their misfortune, did not survive this catastrophe. Devin's full concentration is thinking about this disaster.

[Life here on earth is so short like a breath of air.]

{Psalm 39:5 … You have made my days a mere hand-breadth the span of years is as nothing before you. Each man's life is but a breath.}

[Be Afraid, Be Very Afraid]

When Devin died, he experienced something so horrific, to this day it is very difficult to talk about, and it changed his life forever. The true unspeakable terror happened to Devin's four friends, the friends who cannot share their horrific beastly encounters. The friends whose flesh, well let's just say, what's left of their flesh, because it is being continually eaten on, burned or rotting away. They will remain in complete agony and torment for all of eternity.

[The next few chapters of this book are going to go back in time and you will get to know each one of these kids before they died. The second part of this book will make you lose sleep and hopefully get you serious about **God**!

When I say, **Be Afraid, Be Very Afraid**, you are to fear **God**, who can send you to that unspeakable place called **hell**, just for being out of His almighty grace!]

{Matthew 10:28 … Do not be afraid of those who kill the body but cannot kill the soul. Rather, be afraid of the One [meaning God] who can destroy both soul and body in Hell.}

[Be Afraid, Be Very Afraid]

Let's go back twenty-two years earlier. Devin is seventeen and moving to Merritt Island Florida.

THE MOVE

The year is 2004, Devin, an attractive seventeen-year-old, his mother Diane, [even though the hard years show in her face, she is still an attractive middle-aged blonde], his stepfather James and half-sister Bella are moving from Bloomington Indiana to Merritt Island Florida. James is starting a new job at Cape Kennedy as an engineer. The only one excited about the move is James. Devin is so upset to leave the friends he's known all his life.

Devin and James are unloading boxes from the U-haul truck. The tension in the air between the two could be cut with a knife. James has never cared for Devin and Devin knows it. "Grab that larger box to the right," James demands. Devin rebels by grabbing the smaller box to the left. Diane walks up at this time with eight-year-old Bella. "Please you two, can't we all just get along?" Diane stresses.

Not only can you see a defiant angry teenager in Devin but there is also a lot of hatred that has been growing in him for many years. Sadly, Devin is consumed by a lot of negativities and his heart has become hardened with each belittling statement that seems to go un-noticed!

{Psalm 95:7-8... today if ye will hear his voice, harden not your heart...}

[Be Afraid, Be Very Afraid]

WHY IS DEVIN SO ANGRY?

By the very young age of six, Devin was already use to the continuous fighting and arguing between his father and mother. One emotional day, he watched his father who he loved so very much, pack up his things and move out. His parents divorced. Devin could not understand what was happening; he only knew he was broken hearted.

This was a lot to handle for the innocent little guy. When Devin was just seven, his mother met a man named James; the two quickly married and now Devin has a stepfather. Devin's real father {Tom}, not surprisingly came around less and less. When Tom would visit, Diane would approach him out of concern for their son and of course the lack of child- support, which Tom never paid.

When Tom was alone with Devin, he would tell him that he would come around more often, but his mother did not want him to. She only wanted her new husband James around and she wanted James to be Devin's father. Wow, a lot for a little guy. Tom was angry at Diane for divorcing him and going on with her life. The way to hurt Diane was going to be through Devin, this was Tom's immature thinking. How cruel, self-centered and wrong of Tom to lash out this way.

The "Seed" that he had planted inside his own son would soon take root and grow into a strong tree of anger, hatred and rebellion! Tom was the reason for their divorce. His wondering eyes gave way to adultery one too many times.

[Oh, Satan loves Adultery and Divorce!]

{Exodus 20:14 … You shall not commit adultery.}

[Be Afraid, Be Very Afraid]

To add to Devin's misfortune, James his stepfather really cannot stand Devin. It is only but a season, he pretends to care for Devin; the fact that this is another man's child sickens him. {This child is not his blood!} James has never loved Devin and Devin knows it.

Diane gave James the approval to spank Devin, and boy did James find every opportunity to take advantage of this wrongfully given authority. There were constant reasons why Devin was going to get reprimanded or spanked. James would call him "a problem child", always creating chaos, always giving negative correction never positive discipline and never done with love. James's lack of empathy and love has consumed him with coldness towards Devin.

When Diane finally started to see what was really going on between James and Devin, she tried to show James how to correct a child with love, and she tried to protect her son Devin; this caused fights between Diane and James. The problems between James and Devin have never been resolved and have caused a lack of tranquility and harmony in their house.

Diane loves God; she is a good person inside out. She had to give this completely to God; it was too much for her to bear alone. She has a motherly protective nature for Devin her son. Diane knows she is the only one, who is really there for Devin, but she also knows the word of God, and she tries to give her husband respect; the lack of peace in the household at times was all too over-whelming!

{Psalm 55:22… Casts thy burden upon the Lord, and He shall sustain thee; God will never let the righteous fall.}

[Be Afraid, Be Very Afraid]

Diane was not able to protect Devin all the time and his anger for his mother began growing. Devin is angry at his mother for marrying a man who abuses him mentally and physically and for divorcing his father Tom. Diane gives birth to Bella, Devin's half-sister while Devin is only nine years old. His mother is now very busy with a newborn.

[Who is going to protect Devin now?]

Devin learns very well through the years how to rebel and give complete disrespect. James's abuse on Devin continues, he has added some new abuse this time and it is through the constant praise he gives to his daughter Bella. He purposely never gives any praises to Devin. This is why Devin is upset at the world and carries a chip on his shoulder. Now he has moved to a completely strange place with no friends. Going into the eleventh grade is tough enough, but doing this in a new city and new school. "Thanks mom," Devin says sarcastically to himself.

The tension between James and Devin only makes the unpacking more miserable. "Devin, take my car and go to the store and pick up some milk please," Diane suggested. Devin doesn't say a word, hoping to annoy James even more. The keys were in her handbag, he grabs them and goes. The drive to the store is not far, just a few minutes away. This gives Devin some time to calm down and gather his composure. Devin begins to think of his real dad Tom; he hasn't seen him in five years. Last he heard his dad took off to Arizona with a friend in order to avoid paying delinquent child support.

"Why didn't he bring me with him?" Devin thought. To reconcile and live with his dad anywhere would be better than living with James his stepfather.

Devin was beginning to resent his whole existence.

When he reached the store he notices a kid about his age, outside leaning up against the brick wall smoking a cigarette. It looks as if this young man works there, his shirt suggested it. Devin parks the car and gets out. He walks right by the young man and doesn't say a word. While exiting the store with milk in one hand and a coke in the other, Devin stops abruptly.

He glanced at the young man to make conversation. "Is there anything to do in this town?" Devin asks. "Well, the Cocoa Beach pier is a pretty good place to hang out," the young man suggests. "Hey my name is Devin, as you can tell I've just moved here," Devin says with a smirk. "Hey I'm Johnny," the young man introduces himself. "So what's so great about the Cocoa Beach pier?" Devin questions. "A lot of kids our age and a lot of bikinis," Johnny answered with a grin.

Devin stayed and talked with Johnny for about fifteen minutes, Johnny's break was up and he had to get back to work. It was nice talking with someone his own age and Devin knew in the future there would be many more pleasant conversations with Johnny.

The Beach

Devin wondered should he return to the emotional drama at his house or try to find this Cocoa Beach pier. Devin being the young man who thrives on rebellion and resisting authority made up his mind quickly; off to the pier he went. The only directions he remembered, take a right off Courtney onto a major intersection called 520 causeway, go straight until you get to the end then go left, you'll see it down on the right.

Devin's a little nervous he doesn't know the area, he doesn't know where he's going and hopes he'll be able to get back home. It's a Saturday afternoon and the traffic seems very busy. Traffic wasn't this busy in Bloomington Indiana; of course, being a college town it was only during the week when you would experience a busy traffic flow. Devin wondered what the high school was like there; it was just a little more than a week before school started. Devin needed to register in a few days.

Devin passes restaurants and the mall, wow this place has everything. Devin had never seen so much water before, it was all so serene. The most water he had ever seen was at Lake Monroe in Indiana.

The beach in Bloomington was Lake Monroe and now for the first time ever Devin was going to see what a Florida Beach looks like, for that matter what an ocean looks like. Devin just crossed the last intersection and noticed a lot of surf shops; they were everywhere, he cannot believe how crowded this place is. Weekends are crazy he thought.

Devin is finally at the Cocoa Beach Pier, and it was packed. He has to drive further down just to find a parking place. Nervous, he decided to stay in the car for a few minutes just to see what everyone was wearing. Observing, Devin witnessed a few kids getting out of their cars and walking to the beach. This gave him some satisfaction to his curiosity. Devin was in a tee shirt, blue jean shorts and tennis shoes, wow, he looked like a complete tourist and he knew it. The dominant dress for girls of course, bikinis and guys wore swimming trunks, also known as baggies. The shoes were flip-flops, also known as slaps or no shoes were worn at all.

Devin trying not to look so obvious took off his shirt and shoes; he was a little embarrassed by his white feet. The blue jean shorts would have to do. As he started walking to the beach, Devin was amazed at all the kids. Teenagers everywhere, this was the teenage jackpot! Johnny who he met at the store earlier had guided him in the right direction. As Devin approached the beach, he leaned against the wooden rail to observe everything before walking onto the sand. Even though he was in blue jean shorts, it did not stop the looks he got from several girls, he was a very attractive toned young man.

Wow! The ocean is absolutely indescribable. This was the most beautiful sight he had ever experienced. Devin was speechless. The different colors of blue were fantastic. There was not a cloud in the sky, yet you felt a continuous breeze. The different shades of light blue from the sky touched the different shades of a deeper blue in the ocean. Like true love that would never separate, was the sky and ocean. "Gods favorite color must be blue," Devin thought. He never saw such a huge mass of water that never ended.

After leaning against the wooden rail for a few minutes trying to take in all the beauty, Devin sees a place under the pier, in the shade to sit. The sand on his feet felt nice, not like walking on dirt. With each step the sand would surround his feet and go in between his toes. The summer heat made the sand hot, very, very hot and Devin's virgin white feet felt it.

Not wanting to look like a complete tourist or idiot, he walked extremely fast to his destination. Underneath the pier at the very end next to a piling was a nice shaded spot. Above, the pier itself was made up of many small shops. At the very end of the pier was a restaurant, where you could sit inside, or outside. The inside had more of a dress code requirement and the outside was more relaxed. Devin again looked at the ocean, and enjoyed watching the seagulls run along the edge. Girls were in bikinis everywhere, sunbathing or reading magazines.

Looking out at the ocean there were many surfers, and Devin was amazed at how a small bump in the water, in the distance, could end up being such a huge wave in the end. The waves came in sets to Devin's amazement. Surfing was a sport he had heard of, and for the first time he was enjoying watching it. "How could the surfers make it look so easy, this is an intense and very dangerous sport," Devin thought.

Many pro surfers were from this area, it would be something if one day, he was able to watch them surf. The continuous breeze off the ocean felt great but what a difference in temperature if you were sitting in the direct sunshine. Some boys were playing Frisbee at the edge of the water. The rolling waves covered their feet, if one boy did not catch the Frisbee, the ocean itself would try to devour and snatch the Frisbee, and you would think the Ocean was joining in the game.

A few other boys in the near distance were skim boarding across the very end of the waves; it was amazing how far they glided. There was a volleyball game higher up in the sand. Devin was very good at volleyball, he would have loved joining in the game but his tender, virgin, white feet would not allow it. There were two girls walking onto the beach, they definitely caught Devin's eye. A gorgeous blonde and a beautiful brunette walked down to a sheet laid onto the sand not far from where Devin was sitting. Wow, he was glad he had not headed home yet. They had been shopping at one of the shops on the pier, you could tell because of the bags they were carrying.

The blonde was the one most appealing to Devin; he tried not to be so obvious with his stares but just could not control himself. Every second he was given to prolong her captivating beauty, was used up with each given glance. In Devin's thoughts he saw complete angelic flawlessness.

His admiration and amazement of the ocean did not touch the beauty he was witnessing. Every one of his senses was activated because of this one girl. The beach was packed with a lot of attractive people mind you, but if Devin had to critique which one stood out, hands down she was the one and only. Catching his stares the beautiful blonde girl looked at Devin and gave a pleasing smile. Devin smiled back and gave a nod with his head.

Devin looked back at the ocean to save his self-respect. Oh no he thought, blue jean shorts, what a complete geek! The brunette started waving at one of the surfers in the ocean, the surfer waved back. The girls were whispering and giggling back and forth. Devin was embarrassed he tried not to stare too long but just couldn't help himself.

The brunette got up and walked to the water, the surfer that she had been waving at was paddling in. Grabbing his surfboard up and tucking it under his arm, was how he carried it in from the water. A kiss was their first response when they were finally together. Devin wondered if the blonde had a guy she was waiting to meet up with. The surfer dude that was with the brunette was tall, dark hair, well built, and very handsome.

It was time for them to go and they started gathering up their things. "I'll meet you at the car," the handsome dark haired young man said. "Wait Alex {this was the young man's name} carry these," the brunette said, as she hands him a few of the shopping bags. "Paige {the brunettes name} would you please retie my top it's loose," the blonde asked? Devin watched her top be retied and wished he was the one assisting in the emergency. She knew Devin was watching and toyed with his emotions. Her backside was facing him as she bent over while putting on her shorts purposely to tease him.

{Matthew 26:41 … "Watch and pray so that you will not fall into temptation. The spirit is willing, but the body is weak."}

[Be Afraid, Be Very Afraid]

"Every part of her was flawless," Devin thought. As she was leaving, she gives one last smile his way. Devin tries to show a tough guy outer surface, he grins, and gives one final interested nod. Glad she did not get to witness the dreaded tourist blue jean shorts exiting off the beach. However, he was completely devastated over the fact that he did not even know her name; Devin wondered if he would ever get to see her again. The Cocoa Beach pier was going to become a regular hang out. Devin had been there long enough; it was time to head home.

Diane Meets Keri

James had been grumbling at Diane for a while, since Devin did not return home quickly. James's dominant, negative, controlling, and moody personality can be so overwhelming and frustrating for Diane. Devin never does anything right in James's eyes. James can be such a terrific father to Bella, why is he so unfair and cold towards Devin?

This has already given Diane an unnecessary stomach ulcer, which acts up more during situations like this, along with other medical problems. She is concerned about Devin's long absence in a new and unfamiliar area. Diane trusts her son and believes in him, even if James does not. Devin has disappeared many other times to clear his head and gather his thoughts.

James was about to bring up Devin one more time, and Diane knew it, she was about to explode herself. The tension escalated in the room and suddenly relief came with a soft knock at their front door. Diane went to the door with little Bella following behind her. Bella was such a beautiful little eight-year-old girl, big blue eyes and blonde curls, so innocent and precious. She carries her little doll in her arms and acts like she is the doll's mother.

When Diane opens the door, she is greeted by a friendly face. "Hello my name is Keri, I'm your neighbor, and I brought you this basket of fruit to welcome you to the neighborhood. This is my son Caleb and he is eight," say hello Caleb. Caleb was bashful and hid behind his mother. Diane was elated to see a friendly woman who looks close in age. It was a plus that they both had children the same age. "Praise God," Diane thought. "Please come in, would you like a cup of coffee," asked Diane. "That would be wonderful, thank you," Keri responded.

They went inside and Diane led Keri towards the back porch, the house was still a complete mess, due to the unpacked boxes that were everywhere. "It will be nicer if we sit outside on the back porch, there is a Jungle Jim in the back yard for the kids," suggests Diane. Keri was gathering her thoughts on the newly moved in family and was very pleased, Diane has made her feel so welcomed and comfortable; also Bella and Caleb were playing well together. The backyard was oversized; a four-car garage was located at the back of the house to the right.

Unless you were in the backyard you would never have known the garage was there. A huge oak tree was in the distance with a tire swing, this is where the kids were playing. The neighborhood they moved into was an older one; their house however was one of the largest and nicest homes. The house sat on four lots instead of just one. Diane returned with the coffee, "I hope it's not too late or too hot for coffee. Keri replied, "This is fine thank you." Both mothers stared at their children for a few moments, watching how well they played together; this was enjoyable.

It was a warm day and the shaded porch gave both women comfort. "I have another son age twelve," Keri said. "Me too, but Devin is seventeen," Diane responded. The two women talked a while; Diane was really enjoying her new girlfriend. She found out Keri was divorced and had moved here to take care of an ailing grandmother.

During their conversations Keri had invited Diane to her church. It was a great church not far from where they lived. The Pastor was down to earth, Spirit filled, and not long winded. Diane asked about the worship music, that was her favorite. Keri insisted the worship and the youth group was both powerful and incredible. Diane was feeling such a sense of relief and peace, when not much earlier she was ready to scream. She agreed to visit Keri's church.

Diane heard arguing and she realized it was James and Devin. Devin had made it home from the store; hopefully he had remembered to bring home the milk. Embarrassed she apologized to Keri for the yelling and cursing that her new friend was witnessing. Keri knew it was time to go. Diane looked concerned and was quick to accompany Keri and Caleb to the front door. James and Devin were yelling and cursing at each other, they did not care who was there.

Keri was glad to have met Diane but not happy with what both eight-year-old children were hearing come out of the mouths of adult men.

{Romans 3:14 … the unrighteous are full of cursing and bitterness.}

[Be Afraid, Be Very Afraid.]

Keri smiled at Diane and gave a comforting and not judging hug while exiting. As Keri walked away, she could hear the arguing with each uneasy step. She felt for her new friend. The hostility and strife in that household was all too familiar to Keri. Even though Keri has been married only once, her oldest child was not her husband's. Her son Matte was the only beautiful thing that came from a date rape. Matte was only one when Keri got married. Caleb was born when Matte was four-years-old. Keri's husband was awful to Matte that is why she divorced him. She really does understand the controversy and contention in that household.

When Diane closed the door, she was so frustrated the obvious enormity of this heated argument was so unnecessary and ridiculous. Being the peacemaker that she was, she was able to calm James down and sent Devin to his room to calm down. After a few minutes went by Diane softly knocked on Devin's door and asked if she could possibly enter his room.

"Hey," Diane said softly, "where were you?" "I went to the store like you asked me to and a kid I met told me how to get to the beach so I went to check it out." Still aggravated Devin said angrily, "I did nothing wrong!" Trying to rebuild her relationship with her only son, Diane sits on the end of his bed and asks all about his trip to the beach. Devin reluctantly shares his experience with his mother. Even though Devin was angry at her for divorcing his father and marrying James, he still loved her. Diane asked Devin if they could go to the beach together sometimes. Devin struggles with a nod, to say yes, but gives in.

Diane feels this is the perfect opportunity to invite Devin to church tomorrow. "I've been invited to attend a new church, I was told it was really good, with a lot of teen-agers, let's go to the beach after church tomorrow Devin, please"

Diane asked? Frustrated, Devin answered quickly, "Mom no, I'm not going to church tomorrow with you, not tomorrow, I want to head back to the beach and be by myself, please understand, I really enjoyed the break and school is starting soon."

Diane hugged her son and explained she completely understood and wished that she had more time to herself. "Devin," Diane said firmly, "you need to take time out of your busy schedule to know God; he wants you to know his presence; this is so very important, promise me Devin, if I enjoy this new church, will you go with me some Sunday?"

{Psalm 51:11 … do not cast me from your presence or take your Holy Spirit from me.}

[**Be Afraid, Be Very Afraid**]

Devin responded, "Ok Mom I promise, by the way Mom, can I have some money to buy a pair of swimming shorts, I saw a lot of surf shops, and I looked like such a tourist dressed the way I was, please Mom!" Diane agreed since they were bonding so well together. She let him know that her, James and Bella would take James's truck, and he could drive her car.

"Thanks mom," Devin said with some gratitude and appreciation. Diane hugged her son one more time. Devin was hoping the blonde girl that gave him so much excitement would also be at the beach the next day and possibly, he would find out her name.

CHURCH

Sunday morning came; Diane woke with excitement but was also a little nervous about visiting a new church. James decided he did not want to attend, he would rather work in his garage, and there was still a lot of unpacking that needed to be done. Devin was still asleep when Diane and Bella drove off to church. They left plenty early and while on their way to church a young man who was not patient with his driving almost hit Diane and Bella head-on while he was trying to pass another car. Diane swerved off the road. She was shaken up but bowed her head and thanked God for His faithful protection over them. Diane drove the rest of the way at a slower pace to make sure they got there safely.

The church parking lot was already full. Keri waved for Diane to join her, and showed her Bella's classroom. Bella and Caleb were in the same classroom together, this made Bella a lot more comfortable. It was nice being greeted with a smile and a hello as they entered the building. Keri started introducing Diane to a few people. Her preferred sitting area was closer to the front and in the middle of the three sitting rows.

Diane was so energized and wound up completely thrilled about the music starting. To worship and Praise God was so badly needed in her life and spirit. The worship started and was filled with excitement, indescribable and uncontainable. This was a Spirit-filled church! "Praise God," Diane thought. She stood as everyone did and raised her hands to praise like a little child going before her breathtaking, awesome God.

{Matthew 18:3 … Unless you are converted and become as little children, you will by no means enter the kingdom of heaven.}

[Be Afraid, Be Very Afraid]

The **Holy Spirit** was there, Diane felt him, her heart wished the beautiful music and the awesome worship would never end. Tears welled up in her eyes and began rolling down her face. Her eyes stayed closed and she whole heartily worshipped her Lord and Savior. She knew most of the songs they played, because of her previous Spirit filled church.

Devin had woken up by this time he was dressed and heading out the door, he did not wish to see James so he was discreet with his exiting. Devin stopped at the store to pick up a drink, his friend Johnny was working. Johnny took a short break and he and Devin enjoyed another conversation. Devin thanked Johnny for sending him to the Cocoa Beach Pier, "Wow talk about a lot of hotties," Devin commented.

Johnny had his smoke and Devin explained he was heading back to the beach for the day. His mom had handed him seventy dollars and he was excited to see what he could purchase. Off he went. Back at church, worship had just ended and everyone was seated. The beginning prayer was pleasant. Diane always loved to see a grown man praying out loud to God. Her husband James never does and his Bible remains a dusty book on a shelf.

It was like Jesus was really not welcomed or praised in their house, He remains outside their front door with a heartfelt and earnest, continued knocking.

{Revelation 3: 19-21... those whom I love I rebuke and discipline. So be earnest, and repent. Here I am! I stand at the door and knock. If anyone hears my voice and opens the door, I will come in and eat with him, and he with me. To him who overcomes, I will give the right to sit with me on my throne, just as I overcame and sat down with my Father on his throne.}

[Be Afraid, Be Very Afraid]

Diane was a welcome visitor and received a welcome package. Announcements were brief but stressed on buying tickets for a Mel Gibson Film, The Passion of the Christ. A brief portion of the film was shown and more tears ran down Diane's face. Wow, how detailed and descriptive on what Lord Jesus the Son of God went through for her a sinner so that she could have eternal life in Heaven!

{John 3:16-18 … "For God so loved the world that he gave his one and only Son, that whoever believes in him shall not perish but have eternal life. For God did not send his Son into the world to condemn the world, but to save the world through him. Jesus says, "He who believes in Him is

not condemned; but he who does not believe is condemned already, because he has not believed in the name of the begotten Son of God."

[Be Afraid, Be Very Afraid]

The tithing plate was passed around and Diane was happy to give, this seems like such a wonderful church. She knew that when she contributed financially, she was a part of each person's life this church touched.

The Pastor went to the front; to Diane's surprise he wasn't an older gentleman like her last Pastor, but middle-aged and rather handsome. Diane asked Keri where his wife was sitting and she pointed her out. His wife had a soft innocent sweet look about herself. Watching her watch her husband with complete admiration and respect, only women looking for true love's kindred spirits could appreciate.

The Pastor began to speak and would glance at his precious wife as if she was the only backing and support he needed. The Pastor spoke on Ephesians, how we seriously have powerful evil forces working against us, at all times, and how our children are at risk of eternal damnation, families are being completely destroyed.

Everything he was speaking about, Diane felt as if the pastor knew her family situation and he was speaking to her alone. Diane wished that her husband and Devin were right there hearing this powerful intense message. It is by grace we are saved, this is a precious gift from God.

{Ephesians 2:8… for it is by grace you have been saved, through faith-and this not from yourselves, it is the gift of God…}

[Be Afraid, Be Very Afraid]

The Pastor shared that there is an accountable time for everyone to make it to heaven or not, and that God knows that accountable time, he is a just God; you want to make it into Heaven. If you don't make it into Heaven you will be going to hell for all eternity, forever, and ever, and ever!! The Pastor shared how Kenneth Hagin died at age fifteen and had shared how he descended down and down to the gates of hell.

Diane was so heartbroken, the thought of her seventeen-year-old son Devin whom she loves so very much, going to the depths of Hell to be forever tormented, and this was too much too bare! If Devin died right now, she knew he would not make it into Heaven, he was still so angry at her for divorcing his dad. He was angry at James his step father for never loving him as his son, and taking it out on him to the point of being abusive.

Devin was angry at his father Tom for abandoning him. Devin's anger began as a young child, and now has consumed him.

[Satan loves it when you are angry and you do not forgive the person you are angry with!]

{Ephesians 4:26-27 … "In your anger do not sin," Do not let the sun go down while you are still angry, and do not give the devil an opportunity.}

[Be Afraid, Be Very Afraid]

When the Pastor gave an alter call and shared on:

Matthew 10:32, "Whoever acknowledges me before men, I will acknowledge him before my Father in heaven but whoever disowns me before men, I will disown him before my Father in heaven.

Diane needed all the help she could get, and you can't get any better than Jesus the Son, going to God the Father, on Diane's behalf for her son Devin. She was the first one to the front. Women prayed for women and men for men, how appropriate. Diane went to an older woman for prayer, she was glad a lot of compassion and wisdom usually follow the elderly. "Please pray for my son's salvation, he's a rebellious seventeen-year-old teenager." Diane pleaded! The elderly woman gave a comforting smile as if she knew exactly what Diane was going through.

 She began to pray and Diane held her hands tightly. This woman's prayers for Devin's salvation were incredible, Diane felt the Holy Spirit all over herself and she could not stop weeping and trembling. Diane knew this woman had to be a mother herself and more likely a grandmother. Diane had a wonderful first visit and was very happy her friend invited her, she will definitely return.

 Devin is still at the beach, he was able to purchase a pair of baggies on sale, a beach towel and some flip-flops at one of the surf shops. Watching the ocean and the people was enjoyable, but the girl he went there to see again, never showed up. Devin patiently waited all afternoon and into the early evening, he left with some excitement knowing school registration was the next morning.

Chapter 3
THEY MEET

*I*t's Monday morning and Devin is on his way to register for school. He stops for his regular store drink and enjoys another short break talking with his friend Johnny. Johnny had dropped out of school in the eleventh grade, but was able to give Devin some information about the High School he would be attending.

While Devin was on his way to school, he noticed a rather large Church on the right as he drove past. This was the church his mother Diane went to, and wants him to visit with her. There was a saying on the sign on the church that read, No Jesus, no Peace, to Know Jesus, is to know peace!

Devin thought nothing of this saying!

{*Isaiah 59:8 … the way of peace they do not know; there is no justice in their paths.*}

[Be Afraid, Be Very Afraid]

This High School seemed bigger than the High school Devin attended in Bloomington Indiana. There were many kids there also registering for school. Devin just followed where everyone was going; he was led to the school cafeteria. Tables were set up in alphabetical order to register. Devin was not on file yet at the school because he just moved from Indiana, so he had to go to the front office to clear things up. Everything was fine and school would start in a week, so Devin used the time wisely to unpack and finish his room. He thought about the blonde girl often.

Day one of school was a little nerve racking, but exciting at the same time. There was a morning pep rally; all the classes were to go to the gym. Devin sat in the middle of the bleachers. The principle welcomed everyone and gave a brief speech. While this was going on Devin was observing everyone around him. To his surprise, the beautiful blonde girl he had seen at the beach and had thought about so much was sitting a few rows down in front of him. He could not believe it, she goes to the same school he does. This school was looking better and better.

She was sitting next to the brunette, whose name was Paige and the dark-haired boy whose name was Alex, and sitting next to them was an African American boy; Devin did not know his name yet. Devin was so excited to see this beautiful blonde again. Everyone was going back to class and Devin watched her exit the gym; he never took his eyes off her. The first day of school seemed pretty laid back; he was heading to his last period class, which was weight lifting.

To Devin's amazement the blonde girl was in his last class; this was a coed weight-lifting class. The teacher read off everyone's name in alphabetical order; you were to raise your hand, so the teacher could memorize who you were. Devin listened and watched his name was one of the first called because his last name was Chaplin. When he raised his hand, she was staring at him and remembered him from the beach. She gave him a smile and a small hand wave. You would think his heart was going to jump out of his chest.

Jayden Pelky was finally called and she raised her hand. Jayden, Devin thought to himself, her name was as beautiful as she was.

They Date

Jayden hung out with another girl but kept looking at Devin he could tell she was interested in him. The teacher was going over all the equipment for safety purposes. Devin kept looking at Jayden with a slight smile; he was trying not to look so obvious but he was so happy to finally know her name and to have a class with her. Before the period was over Devin was determined to have a conversation with her.

The remainder of the class was students trying out the equipment. Jayden lay on a weight bench to lift some weights; Devin was right there asking if he could spot her. Jayden smiled and said, "Yeah thanks." They talked for the remainder of the class. Within the next two weeks Devin asked Jayden on a date, she gladly accepted. They went to an Italian Restaurant and after dinner, Devin drove Jayden to the beach for an enjoyable evening walk. What a wonderful and beautiful evening it was walking along the beach and holding Jayden's hand. He was with the two most beautiful sights he had ever laid eyes on, Jayden and the ocean.

When they stopped walking, they faced each other. Devin could not hold back, he placed his hands behind her waist and brought her closer to him. Devin politely asked if he could kiss her. He wanted to rush in for a kiss but felt that she was worth waiting for. She placed her hands around his neck pulling the two together and responded with a long passionate kiss.

It was official, they were dating. Jayden had fallen for Devin, just as Devin had fallen for Jayden. Jayden had been telling her best friend Paige about good-looking Devin for weeks but they had never met. Jayden was excited about Devin meeting her friends, the kids she mainly hung out with. Paige her best friend, Paige's boyfriend Alex and Lucky

Paige's foster brother. Their first date was on a Friday night. Everyone was going to the surf contest at the Pier the next day.

Alex, Paige and Lucky were at the beach first. Alex had to get there early to sign up for the surf contest. Jayden and Devin road together. Devin's white feet were already tanned over; you would never know he was not born in Florida, he fit right in. Devin and Jayden held hands the whole time walking onto the beach. They made such an attractive young couple.

This was the first surf contest Devin had watched; this was exciting for him. Alex was one of the first to compete and he placed very well, he would definitely be in the finals.

While all the different groups were competing for finals, Devin and Jayden slipped away for another enjoyable stroll on this beautiful beach. You would think they had been together longer the way they just clicked. Walking past the crowds was the moment Devin wanted, to stop for another delicious kiss was the only thing on his mind. After several kisses, they headed back to watch Alex surf in the final competition. Paige was watching their return, she noticed the way they laughed and held each other's hands; she was impressed with Devin's gentleness.

As they returned Paige hit Alex and said, "Look at how sweet Devin is to Jayden, why aren't you like that to me." Alex smiled and said, "They just started seeing each other, we've been together for nine months." Alex heard the announcement and it was time to compete, so he took off with his surfboard.

Devin noticed the marks around Lucky's wrist and wondered what had happened to cause the marks. Lucky saw Devin starring and grabbed his wrist and said, "I'm getting hungry I wonder what's around to eat, I'll be back." Lucky left for a little while. While he was gone, Paige explained about Lucky's foster parent Miss Kate who had abused him; she was the reason for those scars. Lucky was not gone long when he returned with a pizza. "Where did you get that," Paige asked. Lucky smiled and explained it was on one of the tables at the restaurant on the pier. Lucky always grabbed whatever he wanted; if he saw it and could steal it, he would. They all enjoyed the pizza.

{Exodus 20:15 … you shall not steal}

[Be Afraid, Be Very Afraid]

Alex was doing really well in the contest. It was fun sitting on the beach and yelling for Alex, he had his own personal cheering section. Everyone seemed to like Devin; this mattered to Jayden since she valued their friendships so much. Jayden trusted them more than her judgmental parents, who she was so angry with. She was dreading the day they would meet Devin. Devin could tell Jayden's mind was elsewhere so he leaned towards her and gently kissed the back of her neck, this definitely took her mind off her parents. She pushed herself closer to Devin and he just placed his arms protectively around her.

Lucky jokingly grabbed Paige and wrapped his arms around her to imitate Jayden and Devin. They were all laughing and having a fun time. Alex placed second in the contest. After the contest a volleyball game started, Alex and Devin joined in. Lucky, Paige and Jayden sat and cheered them on. Devin was happy to have Jayden watching him play volleyball and he played exceptionally well. The loudest ones cheering were Paige and Jayden. Lucky stayed for a little while and slipped away only to return with a pretty decent backpack. Paige commented, "You are so going to get caught one day." Lucky just smiled and said, "Today is not that day."

Everyone enjoyed a full day at the beach and they made plans to meet up the next day. Jayden left with Devin in Devin's mom's car and the others road with Alex in his red Thunderbird. Paige was smiling and waving the whole time at Jayden as they drove off; Paige knew her best friend was hit hard over Devin, and she was happy for her.

When Devin got home that evening Diane his mom could tell something was up, he was in a great mood, not even James his stepfather bothered him. "Mom thanks for letting me use your car and thanks for the extra cash, I love you," Devin said. Wow was this her rebellious child, Diane thought and said, "You need to mow the lawn and wash my car for the cash." "Ok Mom, I'll do it first thing in the morning" Devin responded. "Devin, you promised to go to church with me and you haven't gone yet." Diane reminded him. Devin answered, "I will but not tomorrow, I met a great group of friends, Mom I have a girlfriend, you will really like her." Shocked but pleased her son seems so happy she questioned, "A girlfriend"? Devin just smiled and said, "You'll meet her Mom, she's perfect."

Devin went to his room only to pick up the phone and call Jayden; he could not stop thinking about her. James and Diane had been watching the news and a Hurricane was heading their way, they were from Indiana so this was a bit frightening to them. The next day Devin was up early to complete his chores, so he could go pick up Jayden and meet up with the group.

Diane went to church with daughter Bella; she so loved this church and had decided to become a member. To become a member, you met after church and listened as the Pastor shared the importance on this decision. Diane knew she was making the right choice and wanted to become intimately involved with her new church, this was part of what becoming a member meant.

When Devin picked up Jayden, her dad Will followed her out the door to meet Devin. He was not happy, it wasn't Alex picking her up with Paige and Lucky like usual, no this was a single guy he had never met. Jayden's dad was not happy at all, Jayden did not even stay for the full church service at their house. "Dad I've heard it all, I want to go be with my friends, I love you but I gotta go," she said as she jumped in the car. She motioned for Devin to go and not allow her father to continue with the lecture. Devin slowly pulled away trying not to be rude, after all he was dating this man's daughter.

Wow, that was uncomfortable Devin thought. Jayden apologized and explained to Devin how her parents had always controlled everything her whole life, her church, her friends and what she was to wear. She was never to have her own opinion on anything.

Jayden had obeyed her parents and gave them complete respect when she was younger but she refuses to as a teenager.

{Exodus 20:12 … "Honor your father and your mother."}

[Be Afraid, Be Very Afraid]

When Jayden started high school, she decided she was going to be her own person and take control of her life that was when she met Paige and everyone. Jayden pulled a bikini out of her purse and said, "See I hide whatever I want to wear from them." Devin reached for Jayden's hand and held it the whole way, her eyes filled up with tears and she poured out her heart. She shared about the youth groups at churches she was never allowed to attend. Devin felt even closer to Jayden; he realized that they both had sad stories to share about their childhood.

The conversation with the group on the beach was the up- coming Hurricane Charley. How could the weather look so beautiful right now when in just a few days a Hurricane was supposed to hit.

Hurricane Charley

Alex's parents were out of town on business and vacationing, they would be gone for well over a month, so everyone decided if Hurricane Charley was going to hit, they would all go to Alex's house. Alex had a nice house in the upper-class area called the Savannahs on North Merritt Island. It was a nice two-story house with an emergency generator outside the garage. News was the Hurricane was on its way.

Devin was a little surprised at the response towards the upcoming Hurricane. Everyone was excited there was going to be a Hurricane party at Alex's. Alex made sure they had plenty of booze, marijuana, and gas for the generator in case the electricity went out. Paige made sure her mom Holly was going to her sister's home. Holly was fine with Lucky and Paige being at Alex's, she knew they would be safe. This was a well-built home. Diane was comforted to know that where Devin was going, there would be an emergency generator. She however did not know there would be no adult supervision.

Jayden did not tell the truth about where she would be staying during the hurricane; she lied to her parents and said she was going to stay with Lucky, Paige and Paige's mother Holly. Devin's parents were unfamiliar with Hurricanes, so Keri their neighbor brought Diane to the store to purchase the necessary supplies.

It was early into the evening when the weather started to change. The waves were huge, Alex was tempted to go surfing, but Paige talked him out of it. This was Devin's first experience with a Hurricane and the news said it was a category four, which was a very strong and dangerous Hurricane. The Hurricane was currently in the Gulf of Mexico, which was the opposite side of the state from the kids and projected to make landfall by the evening.

Lucky made sure he brought his tarot cards for entertainment; he also brought a Ouija board for some spooky and creepy fun. Paige of course had her crystal. Jayden was just happy to be with Devin through this. Alex was happy he would have another evening of sexual activity with Paige. They both were far from being virgins; they think nothing of being promiscuous. They have both been with many other partners sexually.

{1 Thessalonians 4:3-6 ... It is Gods will that you should be sanctified: that you should avoid sexual immorality; that each of you should learn to control his own body in a way that is holy and honorable, not in passionate lust like the heathen, who do not know God. The Lord will punish men for all such sins.}

[Be Afraid, Be Very Afraid]

Unlike Alex and Paige, Devin and Jayden are still virgins. Jayden was waiting until marriage or the person she felt she wanted to spend the rest of her life with. Devin dated a few girls but was never flipped over any of them like he was Jayden.

It's evening now; everyone is on the back porch watching the intensity of the wind and rain. It is incredible, the news said Hurricane Charley has made landfall around Fort Myers and has slowed down some but is still very strong. Even though it came in on the opposite side of the state, if you were watching the news the whole state looked completely covered. It looked like a huge hand beating down on little Florida. The north wind of a Hurricane always seems to be strongest; this was what the kids were experiencing.

The electricity went out and Alex started the generator just for appliances and one light. Since the generator did not power the whole house, it was time to light some candles and play the creepy Ouija board. All the kids were drinking and Alex passed around a joint to smoke. The wind and rain were so strong you would think it was trying to demolish Alex's home.

Paige and Lucky were the ones playing the Ouija board; they both had their hands on the guiding needle. Paige asked the question "Is anyone going to die because of the Hurricane?" The needle pointed to yes. "Are we all going to die," Lucky asked? The needle quickly pointed to yes. Everyone was a little freaked out.

"Wait a minute, you didn't ask if it was because of the Hurricane," Jayden questioned? "Are we going to die because of the Hurricane," asked Paige? The needle pointed to no. "Everyone eventually dies you guys," said Jayden. Lucky really did not believe the next question he was asking. "Are you a demon from hell," asked Lucky. Lucky was trying to freak everyone out since the electricity was out.

The movement from the needle point's straight to yes. Paige looked at Lucky like he was moving the needle himself. "I'm not doing this on my own," said Lucky. "Will we meet you in hell," asked Lucky? This time letters were being spelled out, the letters read, SOON! Alex laughed and said, "That's where all my friends are going to be, anyways it will be like one big party in hell."

[Hell is nothing to joke about!]

[Sadly, the Bible describes these kids as wild waves or wandering stars and they will be in darkness forever.]

{Jude 1:13 ... They are wild waves of the sea, foaming up their shame; wandering stars, for whom blackest darkness has been reserved forever.}

[Be Afraid, Be Very Afraid]

Devin was holding Jayden and Jayden said, "You know I do believe in Heaven and Hell." Paige laughed and said, "You have never talked about religion since I've known you." Jayden said, "I know I'm angry at my parents for shoving it down my throat, I plan on getting my life right with God one day, maybe when I have my own family."

[Get your life right with God, Now!]

Alex said, "Why it is so much more fun being bad, too many rules for being good, and speaking of being bad." Alex grabs Paige's hand and heads to the bedroom with a candle. Everyone knew where they were going and what they were going to do. Paige smiles at Alex and willingly goes with him.

[Paige and Alex think nothing of sex outside of marriage. They also do not believe there will be consequences to pay for their sexual sins against God]

The body is not meant for sexual immorality but for the Lord!

[Sexual immorality is a desired temptation that is always before us. In movies and on television, sex outside marriage is treated as a normal, even desirable part of life, while marriage is often looked down upon and shown as confining and lacking excitement.

We can even be looked down on by others if we are suspected of being pure. However, God does not forbid sexual sin just to be difficult. God knows its power to destroy us physically and spiritually. No one should underestimate the power of sexual immorality. It has devastated countless lives and destroyed families, churches, communities, and even nations. Great people in the Bible were brought down because of sexual sins.

God wants to protect us from damaging ourselves and others, and so he offers to fill us-our loneliness, our desires- with Himself. The awesome Spirit of God! Christians are free to be all they can be for God, but they are not free from God. God created sex to be beautiful and essential ingredient of marriage, but sexual sin-sex outside the marriage always hurts someone. It hurts God because it shows that we prefer following our own desires instead of the leading of the Holy Spirit.

It hurts others because it violates the commitment so necessary to a relationship. It often brings disease to our bodies. In addition, it deeply affects our personalities, which respond in anguish when we harm ourselves physically and spiritually. Sexual temptations are difficult to withstand because they appeal to the normal and natural desires that God has given us. Marriage provides God's way to satisfy these natural sexual desires and to strengthen the partners against temptation. Husbands and wives become one.

Married couples have the responsibility to care for each other; therefore, husbands and wives should not withhold themselves sexually from one another, but should fulfill each other's needs and desires.]

{1 Corinthians 6:13-19 ... the body is not meant for sexual immorality, but for the Lord, and the Lord for the body. By his power God raised the

Lord from the dead, and he will raise us also. Do you not know that your bodies are members of Christ himself? Shall I then take the members of Christ and unite them with a prostitute? Never! Do you not know that he who unites himself with a prostitute is one with her in body? For it is said, "The two will become one flesh." But he who unites himself with the Lord is one with him in spirit. Flee from sexual immorality. All other sins a man commits are outside his body, but he who sins sexually sins against his own body. Do you not know that your body is a temple of the Holy Spirit, who is in you, whom you have received from God? You are not your own; you were bought at a price. Therefore, honor God with your body.}

[Be Afraid, Be Very Afraid]

BACK TO CHARLEY

Lucky decided since it was just the three of them left, he would pull out his tarot cards. Jayden was fine with that; she did not want to be put in an uncomfortable situation with Devin also wanting to head to a bedroom. She knew she was falling in love with him, but she was not ready to give herself to him fully. Devin desired Jayden in an incredible intense way but he was willing to wait until she was completely ready to give herself fully to him, his love for Jayden was growing and she was worth every desired waiting moment.

Lucky shuffles his cards and then asked Jayden to ask a question. Jayden asked, "Have I met my prince yet?" Lucky cuts the cards asked the same question and then had Jayden pick a card from the laid-out deck. The card she turned over was the knight card, which symbolizes prince, love and protection. Jayden looked at Devin and leaned in for a kiss, she knew he was her prince. Happy with her answer Jayden quickly asked another question to the cards, "Will I live happily ever after with my prince?" Jayden sits and smiles at Devin waiting for her answer.

Again, the cards were shuffled and again the same question was asked of the cards. Jayden picked a card from the laid-out deck to give her answer to her question, when she picked her card this time she had a look on her face that was concerning and indecisive, she looked at Lucky for the meaning of this uncomfortable card. Lucky loved the spookiness, this was the worst card in the deck you could have possibly picked, it just escalated the scary windy and rainy dark night; this was the card of death and destruction, a card with a horrible ending. Jayden did not pick the prince card like she assumed she would. Jayden thought she would throw the questions off a little and again asked another question. "Will I marry my prince?"

Devin looked shocked she had brought up marriage, but was happy to know he was the one she was thinking of. Jayden smiled, this will throw off the cards she thought to herself. Lucky again shuffled the cards and again asked the cards the question. Jayden again picked the card that was to be the answer to her question. And again, she pulled out the card of death and destruction, this card shows a horrible skeleton that looked like death. This was horrifying for Jayden. They all just looked at Jayden; she sat back and decided not to ask any more questions.

At this point Lucky was trying to stop the tension in the air, "My turn to ask a question." Lucky jokingly asked, "Am I going to meet my prince charming?" They all knew Lucky preferred same sex relationships. The cards were shuffled and Lucky spread the cards out on the table in front of himself. He reached and picked up a card from the middle of the deck and again to everyone's amazement it was the card of death and destruction.

Devin grabbed the cards and said, "There has to be a lot of that same death card in the deck." Devin was viewing all the cards only to find out what Lucky already knew, "there was only one death and destruction card." "Ok enough with the cards," said Jayden. At this time, it was close to midnight. The wind was still very, very intense; earlier they were able to watch the news, it said the Hurricane would be through the state by the next morning. They opened the back door to see the wind and rain. Debris was everywhere. They could even see a few trees that had been split in two and taken down. This time they could not sit on the porch, the rain and wind came right through the screens. Devin was just holding Jayden. She was standing with her back to him and he had his arms wrapped protectively around her. They were the perfect size for each other; he was a head taller than her.

Lucky went back to the one light in the living room and rolled a joint. The three sat up, smoked marijuana and talked a while. Jayden did not want to go to a bedroom with Devin and he could tell this. There was another couch across from the one they were sitting on. Devin got up and lifted one of the cushions, and saw it was a hide-a-bed, he then went to one of the bedrooms with a flashlight and returned with pillows and sheets; he made a bed with the hide-a-bed and handed Lucky a pillow and sheet for the couch he was sitting on. That was so thoughtful Jayden thought to herself, he's so perfect. They all laid comfortably together in the living room. Jayden was curled up under Devin's shielding protective arm and she fell safely asleep.

Lucky and Devin stayed awake and talked awhile. Devin was not sleepy, if this Hurricane was going to bring down the house, he was going to grab Jayden and get quickly to the bathroom, which was the safest room in the house. The Hurricane did its damage, and was leaving Florida by the time the kids got up. By that time, it was mid-afternoon the next day. The rain and wind were still there, but next to nothing. On the side of Alex's house was his parent's camper; a tree had fallen on it and the Scotty camper looked destroyed. All of the kids stood outside the house on the street to assess the damage.

This was all so amazing, what was an upper-class community just the day before looked completely trashed and had debris everywhere. "Hurricanes are Gods way of pruning the Earth," Jayden said, while looking around. Everyone saw trees that had fallen on roofs, one neighbor's boat had gone through another neighbor's garage and none of the trees within sight had even a single leaf left on its branches. All the trees looked dead. At this time Alex's parents got a hold of him by cell phone and were being up-dated on the damage. They were fine with motor home damage, they had good insurance. They decided to continue with travel plans and they would not return home for six more weeks. Alex's parents informed him where a credit card was hidden if he needed anything.

Alex definitely did not need any extra cash or anything but would take advantage of what his parents again has provided freely for him. Electricity was still out but they were all ok because of the generator his parents had left for Alex. Everyone remained out of school until electricity problems were resolved. Some businesses were able to get electricity quicker to help meet the needs of everyone. Alex informed everyone after everything was back to normal; he wanted to take everyone to a restaurant for dinner, on his parent's credit card of course.

Most of the business's reopened with-in a week and everyone met up to enjoy a wonderful dinner at a restaurant on Alex, actually it was on {Alex's parents.} Everything quickly went back to normal within a matter of a few weeks. You did however still see blue tarps on roofs everywhere mainly on the west coast and also the middle of the state, this meant roof damage. The blue tarps helped prevent more damage to the roofs until they were fixed, but otherwise life went back to normal for everyone. For the kids this meant back to school.

More Hurricanes

It had not even been three weeks since Hurricane Charley, when the news warned everyone that another Hurricane was coming. Hurricane Frances was on her way and this time the Hurricane was going to hit the East coast side, the side they all lived on. The Hurricane was a definite category three so she was still very dangerous and could move up to a category four or become complete devastation, which is a category five.

Devin's parents could not believe another Hurricane; they still did not have their garage damage fixed. Luckily their roof damage on their home was fixed. Alex was the only one excited about the news. He was excited about another Hurricane party at his house. This time with his parent's credit card, he picked up not only booze that a legal aged friend bought for him but also munchies, a nice radio with lots of batteries and lanterns and flashlights. Who needed water that was not a priority?

Alex always had the best marijuana; of course he did he sold it. Also, this time he provided cocaine for the group; he called his hottie girlfriend Paige and let her know he had it all covered, everyone was to just show up and be ready to party. All the kids of course gave the same story as before and when Hurricane Frances was coming, they all went to stay at Alex's and with no parents.

It was afternoon and the partying was going to start early. The cocaine was laid out on the table for everyone to do a line; Devin and Jayden were the only ones to turn it down. Lucky loved doing free drugs and he would try just about anything. "Alex and Paige" wanted the upper of cocaine to stay awake for this Hurricane, but also used alcohol and marijuana as a stimulant and a downer. So even though they were all aware they were doing wrong with the sex, drugs and drinking, it frankly did not matter to them.

{Psalm 51:3-4 ... for I know my transgressions and my sin is always before me. Against you my God, you only, have I sinned and done what is evil in your sight, so that you are proved right when you speak and justified when you judge.}

[Be Afraid, Be Very Afraid]

Hurricane Frances dropped down to a category two when she hit the east coast of Florida. Even though this Hurricane did not seem as strong she stayed for several days beating up Florida, this Hurricane would not move, it was like forty-eight hours before she finally slowly left. It was nice the kids never lost electricity this time; they all realized this Hurricanes worst damage to Florida was a few hours south of them. It was the next county down from them, and families lost electricity for three weeks or more.

Alex, Paige, Lucky, Devin and Jayden all during this Hurricane had a blast the whole time. Devin and Jayden were becoming much closer and they were making out sexually most of the time. They knew they both were still virgins but remaining virgins was becoming very difficult, especially for Devin.

During this Hurricane Jayden and Devin did use one of the bedrooms to further acquaint themselves with each other's bodies, this was the closest Jayden had ever been with a boy and likewise for Devin with a girl. The partial nudity was driving their emotions crazy; it was only a matter of time before they would give in. Alex and Paige again remained in Alex's bedroom and Lucky of course was happy to have a significant amount of drugs. He spent most of the time on the couch that he had claimed at Alex's house. With this Hurricane finally gone, everyone was almost back to their daily routines, when news that another Hurricane was going to hit; it had not even been two weeks since the last Hurricane. Hurricane Ivan was heading up the west coast of Florida like hurricane Charley did.

Ivan was in the Gulf of Mexico and the projection of this Hurricane was going to go across Florida like Hurricane Charley did or go to the top of the state, which would hit the Pensacola area. Ivan did decide to go to the top part of Florida and was a category three to four when it hit. Complete devastation for many homeowners. The President declared a State of Emergency.

To everyone's amazement, one week had gone by since Ivan and another Hurricane was projected to hit the east coast of Florida, in just two more days. This Hurricane was huge, a definite category four that could possibly be a five. The name of this powerful Hurricane was Jeanne; she was definitely going to hit. If she would become a category five this would be catastrophic for Florida. Merritt Island is a large Island, if a category five hit the ocean surge would put everything underwater.

Florida's east coast was still cleaning up what Hurricane Charley and Frances had destroyed, and Hurricane Jeanne was heading in almost the exact same path that Hurricane Frances just hit. This was not good at all. Alex's parents were still gone and he could not really leave the state. Watching the news, you saw traffic backed up as far as the eye could see; you could not get gas anywhere. Due to the closeness of all of these Hurricanes, the gas pumps were literally out of gas. Devin's parents were ready to move back to Indiana, this was their first year here. If Diane did not love her Church and her new best friend Keri so much, she would have insisted that they move back.

Devin was glad to know that they would not be moving back to Indiana, he could not imagine a day of not being with his precious beloved girlfriend Jayden. A lot of people had to ride out this Hurricane, they could go nowhere. Again, Devin's parents allowed Devin to go to Alex's for the Hurricane and again they did not know he wasn't supervised. Paige's mother Holly again went to her sisters and Lucky and Paige went to Alex's. Jayden's parents were not as easily convinced as the last three times to let her go to Paige's mom's home. She started getting angry and yelling at them that she hated them.

Jayden's tongue was lashing out and yelling horrible hurtful things to her parents and she was not going to stop until she got her way she wanted to be with Devin and her friends.

{James 3:6 … the tongue also is a fire, a world of evil among the parts of the body. It corrupts the whole person, sets the whole course of his life on fire, and is itself set on fire by Hell.}

[Be Afraid, Be Very Afraid]

Jayden's persistency caused her parents to eventually give in to her. They had to board up the house and prepare for the upcoming, dangerous Hurricane that was going to hit Florida; this was all so exhausting since this was the fourth time. Jayden was excited to get her way and Paige and Lucky were heading over to pick her up. Jayden's parents again thought that Jayden was staying at Holly's home with Paige, not at Alex's with her boyfriend Devin. They had no idea what their daughter has been seriously thinking about; Jayden had decided she was going to give herself completely to Devin this time; she was going to fornicate with him.

She was deeply in love with Devin and already felt they would be together for the rest of their lives. Devin was gentle and had a lot of patience; he loved Jayden with his whole heart.

First Love

All the necessary Hurricane survival needs were purchased again by Alex. Alex made sure they had booze, drugs, munchies and gasoline. Looks like it's time for another Hurricane party. This Hurricane seemed to be the most dangerous out of the four for the kids. It was very strong and has the possibility of hitting them directly. Florida was seriously damaged by the last three Hurricanes. Hurricane Frances had hit the east coast and stayed for so long that she left a substantial and considerable amount of damage.

Hurricane Jeanne was subsequently following the exact same path as Hurricane Frances. This was not normal for two strong Hurricanes to hit the same area in Florida. Imagine hitting a bug but only crippling it, this was the first Hurricane; the next Hurricane was going to smash it, this was the second hurricane. Early into the evening the weather again started showing signs of the up-coming Hurricane Jeanne. Jayden at Alex's house this time enjoyed drinking alcohol, and smoking some pot with everyone; she wanted to make herself feel a little more relaxed, when she gave herself for the first time to Devin.

This time she knew she was going to lose her virginity. Devin could tell something was up, the last three Hurricanes' Jayden stayed on the alert. Devin knew then she did not want to get into a position that was sexually uncomfortable; Devin completely respected and loved Jayden. Jayden grew up with her parents instilling in her you did not have sex until you were married; sexual relations was only to be with one man, her husband. Unlike Jayden's friend Paige who is promiscuous and has thought nothing of her many sexual relationships throughout her life.

Jayden's decision to lose her virginity and give herself to Devin was a decision she had been thinking of for a while. Like Adam and Eve were recognized in the very beginning as husband and wife. Jayden justified her decision to give herself to Devin, after all she was going to spend the rest of her life with him, who needs a piece of paper; Jayden loves Devin.

{Genesis 4:1 … Adam lay with his wife Eve…}

[Be Afraid, Be Very Afraid]

[Note: There is an important point to make here, even though Jayden believes in her heart she is doing nothing wrong, having sexual relations [**fornication**] outside of marriage is wrong, they are young and not married, and will hurt God and hurt themselves, and bring their sin to their future spouse.]

[Example: A young girl I knew was nineteen years old and a virgin when married, she had saved herself only for her husband. She was so in love with her husband they were still on their honeymoon when one afternoon while walking through the market she briefly left her husband's side to grab a few things they needed.

Upon her return she saw her beloved husband talking to an attractive young girl, she quickly went to his side and stood there anxiously waiting to be introduced as his wife, she was so proud of that fact.

Her husband and the attractive women continued their conversation, this young innocent wife was never even looked at, she felt as if she wasn't even there and purposely ignored. Her husband's complete focus and smiles was for this stranger, another woman she had never met before. Their conversation lasted a few more minutes and they hugged and said their goodbyes.

The transparent wife remained silent and speechless; this was more than just rude she thought. When the brown-haired attractive girl left the young wife looked at her husband and asked who that woman was and why didn't he introduce her. The husband went to his defense, "Oh I'm sorry that was Kim we use to be engaged." The young wife asked if they have had sex, he smiled and proudly said, "Of course."

She was so heartbroken; she knew he didn't introduce her as his wife, because he didn't want to. Her husband's past sin with this stranger hurt the innocent new wife; she knew exactly what her husband had done sexually with this girl and no longer felt special.

Sexual relations are the most intimate you can be with anyone. Sadly, this young wife met many more of his sexual encounters as the years went by in their marriage and each one contributed to heartache. The wife realized she was lucky not to have contracted a disease from her husband. It is better to refrain from sex [**fornication**] until you stand before God and man and join in holy matrimony. Let the Spirit of God fill you and meet all of your needs. **God only wants the very best for us.**]

Back to our story:

As the Hurricane continued the wind and the rain again was very intense. The kids were all watching the news and they realized the worst part of the Hurricane was going to hit the hardest an hour south of them. This was almost the exact same path Hurricane Frances had taken. That poor area would be demolished, many homes would be lost. The kids however were excited they would more than likely not even lose electricity. It was going to be another wild and crazy party time. They all played several card games and watched some movies together. Paige had drunk too much and was feeling sick; Alex had to help get her to bed. Lucky of course was wasted and just chilling on his usual spot on the couch with lots of munchies.

Jayden was feeling the effects of the wine she had been drinking and pot she was smoking; her young youthful body was feeling very aroused. She grabbed Devin's hand and headed for the guest room they had used during the last hurricane.

{Ephesians 5:15-18 … be careful, then, how you live--not as unwise but as wise, making the most of your time, because the days are evil. Therefore, do not be foolish, but understand what the Lord's will is. Do not get drunk on wine, which leads to sin. Instead, be filled with the Spirit of God.}

[Be Afraid, Be Very Afraid]

When Jayden entered the room, she was feeling a bit tipsy; she turned to Devin and began kissing him. Off their shirts went, he had also been drinking, this added to an uncontrollable and unmanageable state of mind. When they lay on the bed Jayden had only her panties on. They were very out of control with each other, and the drugs made it easy for both of them to give in to fornication. There was no holding back this time. Devin's patience was no longer there.

They were each other's first love, and they lost their virginity to each other. They laid the remainder of the night with no guilt, in each other's arms. The howling of the wind and rain did not bother them at all; they never wanted to be apart or separated. The next morning when they woke, they were still naked in each other's arms only to repeat their sexual desires.

When Paige saw her best friend the next afternoon, she knew her friend had had sex with Devin. Paige hugged her friend and smiled with a [your so busted] smile. "Time for a girlfriend potty break,"

Paige blurts out; she wanted to know all the details. Jayden shared her intimate information with her best friend. Paige was on birth control and informed Jayden that she was able to get hers for free at the health department. Jayden agreed she would make it a priority and get on birth control pills to be safe from getting pregnant.

    Devin watched as the two girls returned, he smiled at his beloved Jayden; he knew he was the topic of conversation. Jayden had become Devin's world. Devin and Jayden could not hold each other enough the rest of the day. There was a different connection between the two of them now and everyone could see it and thought it was cool.

[We must not accept the behavior of sin. Love the person, hate the sin! We are to be separate from the world!]

{1 John 2:15 … Do not love the world. If anyone loves the things of the world, the love of the father [God] is not in him. For everything in the world--the cravings of sinful man, the lust of his eyes and the boasting of what he has and does-- come not from the father [God] but from the world. The world not its desires pass away, but the man who does the will of God the father lives forever.}

[Be Afraid, Be Very Afraid]

Part 2
LIFE IS FORGOTTEN IN HELL

Chapter 4
FINAL DAYS

Everyone was trying to get back to normal since the Hurricanes in the Merritt Island area, most of the state of Florida however still had a lot of damage to be taken care of. The group has returned to school. It has been three weeks since the last Hurricane hit, which was the end of September, and it is now October there will be an upcoming Halloween party at school and everyone is really excited.

Paige's favorite holiday was Halloween this is the night known for horror, witches and death, Satan's night Lucky and Paige loved everything about it. They were very excited about what costumes they would be wearing. The Halloween party was coming up on Saturday night but Friday night was an important Football game at the school.

Alex was the quarterback for the team; sounds like another weekend full of fun and adventure for the young group. Devin's mom Diane finally met Jayden and was very pleased with her son's choice. Jayden was well spoken very polite and beautiful; Jayden bonded very well with Diane. Devin didn't want to leave them together talking for very long; he knew his mom would start talking about God. Diane asked Jayden if she attended a church anywhere.

Devin comes walking into the living room to join the two and said, "Oh no here it comes." Diane responded, "Would you guys please go to church with me on Sunday?" Out of respect Jayden asks, "Where do you go?" "I have a wonderful church, a lot of kids your age go there; the church is only a few miles from here," Diane answered. Jayden told Diane she has friends that go to that church but her father reads from the bible on Sunday mornings for her entire family and he has never allowed her to visit other churches. Diane didn't understand why Jayden wouldn't be able to visit other churches but was glad she was taught the Bible. Jayden politely told Diane that she would again ask her parents if she could visit Diane's church.

Jayden knew she had no intention of going to Diane's church; she was trying not to attend church at her own house with her own family. Jayden has been leaving earlier and earlier from her families Sunday service, she was becoming selfish with her time and her heart was becoming hardened and bitter towards her parents and God.

{Hebrews 3:7-8 … so, as the Holy Spirit says: "Today, if you hear His voice, do not harden your hearts…}

[Be Afraid, Be Very Afraid]

Devin spoke up, "Mom, I love you but we have to go, we are meeting everyone at the mall and hit a movie." Diane and Jayden hugged good-bye and when they left Jayden just raved at how cool his mom seemed. "Yeah, ok wait till you meet my stepfather," Devin replied with a smirk. Jayden knew her parents would be the most difficult to be around but Devin wanted to meet them. "Ok sexy you can meet my parents next'" Jayden replied as she leaned in for a kiss. On their way to the Merritt Square Mall, Devin suggested a drink, since they were passing the store.

While at the store Devin asked if his friend Johnny still worked there, he hadn't seen him the last several times he was there. "Hey I'm sorry man you didn't hear the news, Johnny's dead he hung himself," the worker replied. Devin asked, "What happened?" "He was very depressed, he never got over his parent's separation and when his girlfriend broke up with him, he must have felt like he had no one. It all must have been too much for him, sorry man," the worker answered.

Jayden could tell this was emotional for Devin she put her arm around him for support as they left the store. Devin kept thinking about Johnny this was the first kid he talked to when he moved here; he wanted Johnny to meet Jayden his girlfriend. "Wow how could anyone be so depressed that they would end their own life, wasn't anyone there to help him." Devin asked? The young man shrugged his shoulders.

[There are so many depressed teenagers that contemplate suicide daily. If they only knew how much our wonderful God is there to help them, if they would only ask.]

{Psalm 30:10 … Hear, O Lord, and be merciful to me; O Lord, be my helper}

[Be Afraid, Be Very Afraid]

They were on their way to the Mall and Jayden was trying to comfort her boyfriend; Devin was really upset about Johnny, he remained silent. When they got to the mall they met the group at the food court. While they were talking Alex's previous girlfriend walks by and gives Alex a seductive smile.

Alex responded with a flirty smile back, Paige watched it all and was very upset about it, she had nothing nice to say about this girl. "You ain't getting him back you scanky slut," Paige said out loud.

{Ephesians 4:29 … Do not let any unwholesome talk come out of your mouths, but only what is helpful for building others up according to their needs, that it may benefit those who listen.}

[Be Afraid, Be Very Afraid]

Paige was not going to calm down she was still upset over Alex's flirting with his ex-girlfriend. Lucky decided to check out the mall and see if there was anything he could conveniently and easily steal.

{Ephesians 4:28 … He who has been stealing must steal no longer, but must work, doing something useful with his own hands, that he may have something to share with those in need.}

[Be Afraid, Be Very Afraid]

Paige asked Alex to drive her home; her movie night was going to be with her mother Holly and not with Alex. Devin was still upset about the death of his friend Johnny. Since Devin seemed so quiet and it was a school night Jayden suggested a quiet walk on the beach with just the two of them; Devin agreed and off they went. The evening showed signs of fall and the cooler weather only ignited Devin's arm to warm Jayden's chilled shoulders.

The night approaching on the beach was so beautiful Devin and Jayden just sat snuggled together on the sand watching the rolling waves of the ocean, talking softly and laughing together; they were enjoying each other's company so much. This was better than any movie Devin thought; Jayden was successful in cheering him up. The evening went by too quickly; Devin had to take Jayden home. She had to be home by nine o' clock on school nights. When Devin pulled up in the driveway to drop off Jayden, Will, her father was sitting on the porch waiting for her return.

Will had something on his mind and walked to the car to greet Devin. Jayden's father could tell by his daughter's behavior she was in a serious relationship with this boy. Devin was uncomfortable but respectful. Jayden stayed, she was not going to allow her father to be controlling or rude in any way. Will asked firmly if Devin could have dinner with their family that weekend. "Dad, remember I told you there are school events Friday night and also Saturday night," Jayden said. "What about Sunday evening," Will questioned? "That would be fine sir," Devin respectfully answered.

Will was glad he was finally going to spend some time with the young man that has his daughter's heart and replied, "See you Sunday at six, Jayden time to go in the house." There was not going to be a good night kiss for them that evening. Jayden smiled and told Devin she would see him at school in the morning and she obediently went into the house with her father. Jayden was not about to tell her parents she was going to a Halloween party at school on Saturday night. This was a holiday many religious people did not celebrate. Jayden decided her costume would be fun and good not like her best friend Paige who loved the gore of it all.

At school the next day the group talked and decided to meet Friday night at Devin's so they could ride together to the football game. Alex was able to get everyone in the game for free and also the best seats, they knew they had to get there early because Alex was the star player. Jayden and Paige worked together on their costumes; they also made costumes for Alex and Devin. They wanted their boyfriend's costumes to match theirs. This was fun and they were curious to see if their boyfriends would wear what they had worked so hard to put together.

Friday night came quickly; they were all at Devin's house getting ready to leave for the game. Diane, Devin's mother follows the group outside she had just purchased a new digital camera, Diane asked the kids to stand together for a picture. Lucky was at one end, Devin was second from the right with his arm proudly around Jayden then there was Paige and Alex. This photo will be priceless to Devin later on in his life; this is the picture he carries in his Bible.

Everyone was watching Alex play a spectacular game as quarterback for the Merritt Island team; everyone was really enjoying themselves. Alex's ex-girlfriend was a cheerleader, she noticed Paige in the bleachers, and purposely directed dagger like stares at her. Paige spotted her stares and started becoming annoyed. "Paige just ignores her, she's not worth it," Jayden said as she noticed what was happening. "She'd better watch it, I'll rip her hair out and choke her with it," Paige commented angrily.

Jayden reminded Paige, "Paige don't fight tonight you got suspended the last time, besides you've got Alex not her".

{James 4:1-2 … what causes fights and quarrels among you? Don't they come from your own desires that battle within you? You want something but you don't get it. You quarrel and fight.}

[**Be Afraid, Be Very Afraid**]

They were all having such a good time Paige was starting to blow it off. Merritt Island won the football game that night and the coach bought pizza and coke for the team. Paige, Lucky, Devin and Jayden were able to enjoy the benefits of the food and drink since they were with Alex. They all went to Surfs-Up afterwards another fun hangout on the beach. Jayden asked Devin if he would go with her to the hospital the next day her grandmother had eye surgery and was going to be there for a few more days. Devin arrived bright and early to pick up Jayden, they were so crazy about each other when they weren't together they were on the phone with each other almost every day. When they reached the hospital entrance and approached the elevators, Jayden looked at Devin and asked, "Where are the stairs I don't do elevators?"

Devin looked baffled. Jayden explained what happened to her as a child getting stuck in a small bathroom; it terrified her and to this day she cannot be in a small area. Devin hugged her and told her he was right there and he would not leave her side that she had nothing to fear. They still decided to take the stairs; her grandmother's room was on the sixth floor. Jayden and Devin stayed only about thirty minutes with her grandmother.

HALLOWEEN

Jayden and Paige had talked and they would all meet at the Halloween dance that evening. Lucky, Alex and Paige would put their costumes on at Paige and Lucky's house. Devin and Jayden would of course put their costumes on at Devin's. The Halloween party was scheduled to begin at seven o' clock that evening everyone was to meet at school by seven fifteen. Devin had no idea what Jayden had put together for the two of them. Devin had to finish his weekend chores to earn the extra money for the week.

Jayden was dropped off at Devin's by four o' clock he wasn't quite done with his chores so Jayden enjoyed some alone time with Diane and Bella, Devin's mom and sister. Diane told Jayden she was thankful to God for her being in her son's life. She could see a change in her son that was for the better; he did not seem to be as angry as he was when they first moved there.

Diane was glad to sit and chat with Jayden she loved God with all of her heart and wanted to know in her heart that Jayden loved God too. Every time Diane said Praise God while talking to Jayden, Jayden got a knot in her stomach she refused to say Praise God but was polite while listening to Diane. Jayden did not realize how foolish she was being by refusing to have any kind of a relationship with God. Jayden took herself out of the Grace of Almighty God; she listened to Satan's lies and harbored anger and bitterness towards her parents.

[How sad our Father God was!]

TOO LATE

{Romans 1:21 ... for although they knew God, they neither honored Him as God, nor give thanks to Him, but their thinking became futile and their foolish hearts were darkened.}

[Be Afraid, Be Very Afraid]

Devin finally finished his work and went in the house to shower and get ready. Devin came out with a pair of baggies on. "Ok where is my costume and I'd better like it," Devin demanded with a half-smile. Jayden smiled and pulled Devin's costume out of a bag. Jayden had taken a pair of Devin's swim trunks and sewed on a bunch of handmade leaves out of material, the leaves were all different colors. He looked shocked at how small his costume was. She pulled her costume out to show proudly to Devin. One of her bikini tops and a skirt had the same leaf material all over it. Jayden had also made leafy armbands and a crown of leaves for their heads, Jayden's had flowers added to hers. Yes, they went as Adam and Eve.

They both had very nice bodies and looked great in their costumes. Diane took a picture of the two of them before they left for the party. Diane said a silent prayer for them, "Lord be with them and bring them home safe, please my awesome Lord and Savior bring them into your Kingdom, it is through the blood of Jesus I pray Believe and Receive this, Amen." What a cute couple she thought to herself. When they arrived at the school Alex, Paige and Lucky were already there waiting.

Paige's costume took a lot of work, thank goodness her mother Holly was such a good sewer and very creative. Paige was the Cursed Goddess Medusa. They bought a bunch of rubber snakes and glued them in a long tangled black wig she wore. The small Greek robe she wore was both Seductive and Evil with snakes coming off the material and wrapped around her body. Her body and her face were grey, her teeth were pointy and sharp, and she looked evil. Alex's costume was a warrior that had attempted to kill Medusa, legend has it, and if you looked at her you would turn to stone. He wore an above the knee, grey toga and grey body paint and carried a sword. Obviously, he looked at Medusa and turned to stone.

Lucky was Freddy Kruger from the movie Nightmare on Elm Street. Everyone at the party raved about the outfits inside and Paige and Alex won first prize for their costumes. After the party ended, they all met at a more secluded area on the beach. Devin and Alex must have talked before the Halloween party; they both brought sweats for the girls and themselves, some firewood and a blanket with them. The girls took off their make-up and put on the oversized sweats when they stopped at the store on the way to the beach.

The moon was full that night and the warmth of the fire added comfort to a chilled October night. Alex grabbed Paige's hand along with their blanket and they soon disappeared on the beach into the night. Devin looked at Jayden for approval; he also would like to disappear on the beach opposite of Alex and Paige with their blanket. She loved him and was glad they were together. They soon disappeared into the night, this time their make-out time together would be on a blanket on the soft ocean sand. Lucky was left alone with his coat and a joint; he was just fine chilling by the fire.

Dinner at Jayden's

Sunday came all too soon. Jayden knew she was supposed to be home in time for their church service. "Crap I am so going to get into trouble with my parent's; I just don't want to be away from you, just to hear more stuff about God," Jayden commented. Lucky spoke up, "Why bother with Church, there is no God, I can't believe people believe that bull." Paige and Alex just smiled they never had to deal with any church pressure. They agreed with Lucky, there really wasn't a God.

{Psalm 53:1 ... the fool says in his heart, "There is no God."}

[Be Afraid, Be Very Afraid]

Alex and Lucky still had make-up on, they were ready to leave. The group said their goodbyes in the early morning; they would see each other at school the next day. Jayden asked Devin if she could come to his house for a few more hours, she knew she was already in trouble and just didn't want to deal with it. They got to Devin's house before Devin's mom, sister and stepfather went to church. Diane asked Jayden if she had asked her parent's yet about visiting her church and could they both please go this morning with them. Jayden apologized, she did not have the extra clothes and Devin was bringing her home shortly.

Diane is so concerned about Devin's relationship with God; Devin used to go to church weekly with her in Indiana, now he doesn't even acknowledge Jesus!

{Matthew 10:32-33 … whoever acknowledges Me before men, I will also acknowledge him before My father in Heaven. But whoever disowns Me before men, I will disown him before my Father in heaven.}

[Be Afraid, Be Very Afraid]

While Diane was at church, her son was so heavy on her heart she prayed for him silently throughout the entire service. The movie The Passion of the Christ was going to be shown at the church in a few weeks, Oh God she prayed please put it in my son's heart to come with me and see this powerful movie. At the end of the service again she went forward for prayer for her son's salvation, she could tell he was struggling.

{Romans 15:30 … I urge you brother, by our Lord Jesus Christ and by the love of the Spirit, to join me in my struggle by praying to God for me}

[Be Afraid, Be Very Afraid]

Devin and Jayden new they had a few hours of alone time before his parents came back. They timed it perfectly and were gone before Devin's parents returned. Jayden's parents were disappointed with Jayden for missing their Church service, but were looking forward to meeting and examining her new boyfriend that evening for dinner.

Devin was there for dinner by five-thirty and very nervous. Nelly, Jayden's sister answered the door and yelled for Jayden, she rudely did not offer a seat, or a drink, she quickly went to the kitchen to inform her parents he was there. As Devin stood there baffled, Jayden came to his rescue; no one was around yet, so Jayden snuck a quick kiss, she was trying to comfort Devin. Right after that, Jayden's father Will entered the room. "Have a seat young man; what is your name again, Will questioned?" Devin answered politely, "Devin sir." "We are a tight family and Jayden has not been acting herself, could you be the reason?"

Devin looked surprised that Jayden's father had asked this question, he did not know how to answer him. Jayden stepped in and said, "Great dad, I finally found some happiness and you like always are trying to control my life, and run him off, well guess what he isn't going to stop talking to me, like the rest of them did." Devin stays quiet while they continue with this uncomfortable conversation. Nelly came in to inform everyone that dinner was ready. Devin was glad it was dinnertime [wow] the drama his precious first love Jayden was experiencing daily saddened his heart. He did not know how to give her comfort and protection.

At this time, he realized how lucky he was to have such a cool loving mom; he understood now why Jayden fell in love with his mom Diane. Matthew, Jayden's brother just showed up for dinner, everything stopped momentarily. As Devin and Jayden try to walk to the dining room, they could not help but pass Matthew and Will in the hall way. Will did not care who could hear him, he was reprimanding his adult son, "Matthew you are the tail I am the head, the head is in front always, I'm always in control." When Jayden saw her beloved brother being humiliated with harsh words and a finger pointing at him, she was so upset and embarrassed that Devin witnessed this. Jayden hated the way her father always belittled her older brother who she loved so much, this was not Christianity to her.

Jayden became unemotionally quiet and distant throughout dinner. Jayden's mom was worse than her father, Devin felt like he was under a microscope through-out dinner. Unlike his friendly, warm, hospitable mother; the only words Jayden's mom said to Devin was to comment on his long hair. Again, Devin thought wow, she had to be the most unemotional, unfriendly, cold, self-righteous mother he had ever met and then he remembered what Jayden had told him about her mother; she always said this, "Faults in others I can see, praise the Lord there's none in me." Devin wanted to embrace Jayden his love, and put a smile on her beautiful face. They weren't even able to sit next to each other. Will asked Devin many uncomfortable questions; he was doing most of the talking. Devin always just gave a short respectful answer.

Nelly would throw out a praise report about herself, to remind her parents how perfect she assumed she was. Nelly loved that her other siblings looked bad in front of her parent's, it always made her look better; that was all that mattered to [it's all about me] Nelly! Devin gave an excuse right after dinner that he had homework to complete, and had to get home. "I'll walk you to the car," Jayden quickly said. "Thank you for dinner," replied Devin. Will followed them outside and watched them while sitting on his porch. Not even a thank you for coming came out of her parent's mouths. Jayden knew her father was watching so she just leaned in for a hug from Devin and whispered in his ear, "I'll see you tomorrow my love." No kiss again that night.

The Passion of the Christ

The next day Jayden apologized to Devin for an uncomfortable evening with her family. "If I'm with you I'm happy, it's alright," Devin said with a gentle smile. Devin continued, "Hey this Friday night at my mom's church they are showing the Mel Gibson film The Passion of the Christ, I promised my mom I would go. Will you go with me?" At this point Alex, Paige and Lucky walked up, they were all waiting for the school bell to ring. Again Devin says, "Hey you guys my mom bought tickets for everyone for Friday night to watch that Mel Gibson film The Passion of the Christ you're all invited Jayden and I are going." Jayden gave Devin a surprised look she had not committed herself to go yet. Alex looked at Devin and pride fully boasted, "dude your mom is great but I don't think so, I was going to tell you guys about the huge party going on out by my house in the orange groves on Friday night, Paige and I are going; Alex Continued, I'll pay your mom back, you know I have lots of money."

{James 5:1 … Now listen, you rich people, weep and wail because of the misery that is coming upon you.}

[Be Afraid, Be Very Afraid]

    Alex is so full of himself. Everyone always seems to follow him for that. Devin looked at Lucky for his answer. "Hum let me think church or a party with drinking and drugs, I think I'll have to choose to go with Alex and Paige," Lucky sarcastically says with a smile!

{James 4:6 … God is opposed to the proud, but gives grace to the humble.}

[Be Afraid, Be Very Afraid]

Friday came and Diane had been praying very hard for the Lord to touch Devin and Jayden's hearts at church. Devin told his mom they would be there fifteen minutes early; the movie was to start at seven o' clock. Jayden started complaining an hour before they were to meet Diane. Devin really didn't want to go either but he was doing this for his persistent mother. They came up with a lie they called Diane right as she was leaving for the movie, and Devin told her Jayden ate something bad at the food court in the mall earlier, and she could not quit throwing up. Diane was so sad but understood and said she would pray for Jayden.

[If Jayden would have gone to church, she would have asked God to forgive her for being rebellious and hardened, Satan knew this, and the whispers to Jayden and Devin to tell the lie came from him.] [All liars go to Hell!]

{Revelation 21:8 … All Liars will be in the fiery lake of burning sulfur.}

[Be Afraid, Be Very Afraid]

The movie was so intense and powerful about the final days of our Lord and Savior Jesus Christ, Diane could not stop crying. Oh, how she wished her beloved son could have seen this, it was the most descriptive detailed movie of what Jesus Christ went through. The movie was the talk of Christians everywhere and was a hit at the theatres. Diane planned on buying the movie so that she could watch it at home with her beloved son Devin.

The Holidays

Thanksgiving was right around the corner, Diane told Devin to invite the whole group for dinner at their house. She was a great cook and would have dinner ready by one o' clock so everyone could still have dinner with their own families that evening. Everyone thought that was a great idea especially Jayden, she knew Devin would no longer eat at her house; she didn't blame him. Diane also invited her best friend Keri and her two boys.

James, Devin's stepfather wasn't riding Devin so much anymore; everyone actually kind of liked him. Thanksgiving Day came and everyone was having such a nice time. You could be yourself and feel comfortable around Devin's family, Jayden loved this. The younger kids played in the back; Diane of course took lots of pictures and was the best hostess. While Keri was doing the final clean up, Devin, Jayden, Paige and Alex were beginning a game of horseshoes. James was in his garage the younger kids were playing by the huge oak tree in the back of the yard. Lucky was sitting alone on the porch. Diane felt it in her heart to reach out to Lucky she knew he was a foster child who never had parents.

{Psalm 27:10 … though my father and mother forsake me, the Lord will receive me.}

[Be Afraid, Be Very Afraid]

Diane enjoyed sitting with Lucky she gently put her hand on his arm like a mother touching her child. Lucky listened with respect, he really did care for Devin's mom Diane, but there was something that drew people to listen to her, and Lucky did not understand this anointing.

{Psalm 29:8 … The Lord is the strength of His people, a fortress of salvation for His anointed one.}

[Be Afraid, Be Very Afraid]

Lucky and Diane enjoyed watching them play. When they were done Devin suggested everyone enjoy a volleyball game. James even had to join in to make the teams even. The teams were Devin, Jayden, Diane and James against Alex, Paige, Keri and Lucky. It ended up being a very competitive game. The first game Devin's team won, the second Alex's team won and Devin's won the third. Two out of three that was it, they were all tired. What a wonderful and enjoyable Thanksgiving Day they had all had.

Before Alex, Paige and Lucky left Diane said, "Wait a moment I want to give Lucky something." Diane went to her room and came out with a Bible. Diane went to hand it to Lucky; he lifted his hand to receive his gift. Even though Lucky really didn't believe in the Bible he was never given any gifts. Diane gave Lucky a motherly goodbye hug and whispered in his ear read the verse I highlighted where the bookmarker is. And she smiled at all of them as they left.

Alex and Paige were glad they weren't given a Bible, Paige doesn't believe in God and Alex is just too prideful and arrogant.

{Jeremiah 13:15-16 … Hear and pay attention do not be arrogant, for the Lord has spoken. Give Glory to the Lord your God before He brings the darkness…}

Be Afraid, Be Very Afraid]

Keri was next to leave with her two kids and of course a plate of food for her sick grandmother who could not make it. Devin looked at Jayden and asked if she was ready to be taken home. Sadly, Jayden agreed it was close to six and her whole family was waiting for her, even her older sister who she really did not know well. Jayden gave Diane a big genuine hug and thanked her for everything. As she was leaving, she said to Diane, "you know if anything ever happened between Devin and me, you will always be mom to me." Diane smiled and told Jayden thank you. Back to Lucky, he was in the back seat by himself, Alex was driving, and Paige was in the passenger seat.

While no one was looking, Lucky opened the Bible Diane gave him to the bookmarked page, and read what was highlighted.

{Joshua 1:8-9 … Do not let this book of the Law depart from your mouth; meditate on it day and night, so that you may be careful to do everything written in it. Then you will be prosperous and successful. Have I not commanded you? Be strong and courageous. Do not be terrified; do not be discouraged, for the Lord your God will be with you wherever you go.}

[Be Afraid, Be Very Afraid]

Lucky read and with disbelief he smiled and thought to himself, yeah right prosperous and successful, everything I have I have to take for myself; Lucky shut the Bible never to open it again! How very sad for Lucky! The next Holiday that quickly approached was everyone's favorite, it was Christmas. Diane's church was doing a play about the birth of Christ after all that is the reason for Christmas not Santa Clause or presents.

{Luke 2:11-14 … today in the town of David a Savior has been born to you; He is Christ the Lord. This will be a sign to you: You will find a baby wrapped in cloths and lying in a manger. And suddenly there appeared with the angel, a multitude of the heavenly host praising God and saying, "Glory to God in the highest, and on earth peace among men with whom God is pleased with."}

[Be Afraid, Be Very Afraid]

Diane again invited Devin and the group to church; she was not going to give up. Diane decided to invite the group for a Christmas afternoon meal like they had done for Thanksgiving; it had gone so well the last time. Actually, everyone was excited to be invited back, and they all agreed Christmas afternoon would be at Devin's. The week before Christmas was a school dance and it was a formal one. Jayden of course lied and told her parents she was staying the night at Paige's. Alex was the driver in his red sports car. He picked up Devin first; Diane of course comes running out for a hug and said a simple prayer, God protect them throughout the evening.

As they drove off Alex commented, "Devin you're so lucky your mom is so down to earth, it may seem like I have it all, lots of money and the very best of everything; but have you noticed that I don't bring anyone to my house when my parents are home? Dad is usually not there he cheats on my mom I know about it. Mom is wasted by three o'clock in the afternoon on alcohol. Heck, they have separate bedrooms." Alex had never really been that down to earth with Devin; he always seemed to have it all together. It was nice to hear him be honest with Devin; they had a special male bonding moment that evening.

When they arrived to pick up Lucky and the girls, Devin's heart just about stopped when he saw Jayden, she was absolutely beautiful; he placed the flowers he purchased on her wrist. The group looked great and ready for a fun evening. The boys looked great in their tuxes and the girls looked breath taking in their evening gowns. At the dance, Devin never even noticed another girl, unlike his friend Alex. When they slow danced it was like they were the only two people in the room, Devin and Jayden could not take their eyes off each other. They did not realize this would be their last dance together.

Death on Earth was heading their way! Christmas was on a Friday; the kids got out of school on Wednesday. They were all really excited about having two weeks off from school; they didn't have to return until after New Years. Little did they know they would never return!

Life is so short like a breath of air. Devin and Jayden's happiness on Earth will soon end.

{Job 7:7-9 … Remember, O God, that my life is but a breath; my eyes will never see happiness again. As a cloud vanishes and is gone, so he who goes down to Hell does not come up.}

[Be Afraid, Be Very Afraid]

Everyone was at Devin's by noon on Christmas day. Devin's family had opened their Christmas presents early that morning. Diane told everyone Merry Christmas and handed each of them a small wrapped gift. With excitement they opened their gifts. Diane had bought everyone a DVD of the movie The Passion of the Christ. They apologized for not bringing her a gift. Diane said, "Your gift for me is to watch this movie please." They all agreed they would but none of them ever did.

The food looked incredible, James said a nice prayer before they all enjoyed their delicious meal. After everyone finished the main course, Diane comes out with a cake, "Ok time to sing happy birthday." Every one of the kids except Devin and Jayden looked confused. Paige asked, "Whose birthday is it?" "Whose birthday is it Devin?" Diane, questions Devin for the correct answer. Bella, Diane's eight-year-old blurts out that it is Jesus' birthday. They all laughed and sang happy birthday to Jesus Christ; Alex, Paige and Lucky went along with it but thought it was all ridiculous.

The weather was beautiful during the days in the 70's and cooler at night in the 50's. There were no clouds in the sky during this perfect Christmas day. Diane and Keri quickly cleaned up and headed out back for another competitive volleyball game. The time went by way too fast and everyone again said their goodbyes around six o' clock. Diane was the one that walked everyone outside and gave everyone a genuine hug goodbye. Diane had no idea that would be their last holiday together, nor did she know that was the very last hug she would ever give to Devin's dear friends.

[God has tried many times to have a relationship with Paige, Alex, Lucky, Devin and Jayden; God was ignored and not listened to.]

{Jeremiah 13:11… declares the Lord, "to be My people for My renown and praise and honor." But they have not listened.

[Be Afraid, Be Very Afraid]

{Luke 12:5 … Fear God who after killing of body will cast you into Hell.}

[Be Afraid, Be Very Afraid]

{Matthew 25:41… Depart from Me, you who are cursed into the eternal fire prepared for the devil and his angels.}

[Be Afraid, Be Very Afraid]

Chapter 5
NO RETURN

New Years Eve was soon here. Everyone decided to meet at Devin's and drive together in Alex's red Thunderbird sports car. Cocoa Village was closed off for a street party, and a few good bands were playing. James, Diane and Bella had rented a room at the Cocoa Beach Hilton and would be away the entire weekend. With no parents home, everyone was at Devin's by six o'clock; Alex of course brought the booze and drugs and the group was excited about entering into a New Year and they all started drinking early.

They left for the street party by eight o'clock p.m. The evening was chilly, the liquor they consumed added warmth to their under aged bodies. They were losing complete control of their logic. Satan knew this; he knew they would be before him very shortly.

Satan loved knowing he was going to hurt God by hurting our Lords precious children, and they will have to call Satan lord. Satan will devour them with a lot of pain and suffering.

{1 Peter 5:8 … be self-controlled and alert. Your enemy the devil prowls around like a roaring lion looking for someone to devour.}

[Be Afraid, Be Very Afraid]

The countdown to the New Year began and the kids all shouted with the crowd, ten, nine, eight, seven, six, five, four, three, two and one. Happy New Year everyone!!!! Devin grabbed Jayden his beautiful girlfriend and was happy to start their New Year together with a passionate but tender kiss. "Happy New Year I love you Devin," Jayden softly whispered. Their eyes captivated each other. Alex, Paige and Lucky where cheering loudly along with everyone else. The area was packed with people and everyone began heading back to the car; they were trying to beat the traffic.

They were all so wasted, stumbling and laughing all the way back to the car. Alex and Paige were in the front seat, while Devin, Jayden and Lucky were in the back seat. As they got in the car and drove off, Devin and Jayden began making out. "Hey get a room," Lucky says as he is sitting next to them in the back. Devin was excited his parents were out of town and Jayden was again staying the night with him. Actually, everyone was going to sleep at Devin's they had all been drinking a bit too much.

Alex was driving on the 520 Causeway from Cocoa going back to Merritt Island. He was laughing out loud and did not realize how fast he was going. Alex began swerving back and forth he was attempting to pass everyone. No one was wearing a seat belt. Alex was coming down the bridge fast; the swerving in front of the other cars was dangerous and very irresponsible; while in the slower lane a little ahead of them, an innocent vehicle was driving the speed limit; this was an elderly couple also heading to the Merritt Island area.

Alex came up on this vehicle way too fast and when he slammed on the brakes, the car slid sideways; the driver's side of Alex's car hit the back of the other vehicle. This caused Alex's car to go completely out of control. Alex's hands were gripping the steering wheel, as he was trying very intensely to stop an accident. Paige was looking at Alex frantically, with her hand pushing against the dashboard.

Lucky was sitting behind Alex with his window rolled down a little; his left hand was gripping the top part of the opened window. Jayden was in the middle in the back seat; Devin protectively threw his arms around Jayden and pulled her close to him. Jayden frightened, threw her head into Devin's chest. The vehicle was heading for the railing of the bridge and the car drove straight through and began to flip.

As the car was flipping uncontrollably down the side of the bank, rolling to the bottom glass was shattering everywhere. The kids were being thrown around like clothes tossing around in a dryer. The front windshield busted out and both Alex and Paige were thrown from the car. Lucky's left hand was cut in half because he was still gripping the car window. Lucky's door flew open and he was also thrown from the now crushed car.

Devin and Jayden were in critical condition and pinned in the car. A witness called 911 for help. Because this happened shortly after New Years the traffic on the bridge caused a brief delay in emergency medical attention. One side of the causeway had to be completely shut down, police and medics were everywhere. The officers began taping everything off; a few of the kids did not make it, they had died at the scene.

JUDGMENT

When Paige went through the windshield of the car, the hard landing instantly broke her neck. Paige is one of the kids already dead. But Paige is not dead! Remember we will all go where Paige is going.

[It is so important to stand firm with God giving yourselves fully to his work. Don't be moved in the wrong direction.]

{1 Corinthians 15:55-58 … Where, O death is your victory? Where, O death is your sting? The sting of death is sin, and the power of sin is the law. But thanks be to God, who gives us the victory through our Lord Jesus Christ. Therefore, my dear brothers, stand firm. Let nothing move you. Always give yourselves fully to the work of the Lord.}

[Be Afraid, Be Very Afraid]

When Paige left her dead body on earth, her now forever body was taken to a transparent place, a heavenly realm, this place exists between heaven and earth. This place is the place you will go till you find out where you will spend eternity.

[Satan wants to deceive you before you reach this place, once you are there you will never return!]

{Luke 16:26 … so that those who want to go from here to you cannot, nor can anyone cross over from there to us.

[Be Afraid, Be Very Afraid]

Paige slowly looks around at everything; she cannot believe what she is seeing. She pinches herself to make sure this is real, "ouch that hurt" Paige says frantically! Paige is terrified, her heart is about to come out of her chest she is breathing so fast. This place is real. "Oh my God this place is real," Paige screams. There is a lot of activity here. Paige could see all around her in this dark gloomy, terrifying place and what she was witnessing was horrifying.

There were many creatures some not as horrifying as others. Some were enormous in size others smaller, they were all shapes and sizes from thirteen feet to four feet; all of them were evil. In some ways it looked like a command post in this second heaven.

Paige witnessed giant black-eyed soldiers that were in charge they were commanding the smaller grotesque demons on what to do. There were portholes [funnels] that went back to every area on earth; these evil deceiving fallen angels were going back to earth to cause many more of God's children to fall away from Him.

Paige could not comprehend why she understood everything that was happening; she only knew she had a spiritual knowledge of what was going on. She knew Satan was real and this place was his working headquarters.

{Ephesians 2:2 … in which you used to live when you followed the ways of this world and of the ruler of the kingdom of the air, the spirit who is now at work in those who are disobedient.}

[Be Afraid, Be Very Afraid]

[Note: "The ruler of the kingdom of the air" was understood to mean Satan. Satan and the evil forces inhabited the region between earth and the sky. Satan is ruling this evil spiritual kingdom, also are the demons. This place is the place of judgment.]

Paige noticed three demons being ordered to do work on earth, one was the witchcraft demon, the other was the greed demon, and the last one was the suicide demon. The witchcraft demon looked straight at Paige before leaving and gave her a chilling smile and wink as if this was the dreadful demon that visited Paige many times and fooled her; she willingly agreed to his deceit while on earth. Paige's heart is racing so fast. There is no love in this place. Paige noticed the only pleasant thing to look at was huge majestic angels of the Lord, they were equipped with swords and at any given moment they were ready to battle these evil fallen forces. There is a spiritual battle going on and no one is aware of this, Paige thought to herself.

{Ephesians 6:12 … For our struggle is not against flesh and blood, but against the rulers, against the authorities, against the powers of this dark world and against the spiritual forces of evil in the heavenly realms.}

[Be Afraid, Be Very Afraid]

Paige realized she did not make the right choices while alive on earth, this only added to more fear. Where will her permanent home be? While Paige was looking around, she noticed more individuals like herself who must have just recently died. There was a difference though. A few people had beautiful, radiant garments on while many others were completely naked. Paige looked at herself; she was also completely naked and ashamed.

{Revelation 16:15 … blessed is he who watches, and keeps his garments, lest he walk naked and they see his shame.}

[Be Afraid, Be Very Afraid]

Paige noticed a breathtaking person in the distant that was wearing a garment, this person was standing in front of a beautifully lit tunnel covered in flowers that went up to Heaven. The only lighted areas were the few tunnels that lead upward. Paige watched as two demons were antagonizing someone, as these demons got closer to the individual a breathtaking, magnificent angel of the Lord swooped down in front of the person and drew his sword to protect this child of the God from these fallen angels. This was a guardian angel. The demons backed away, they knew this was business for the guardian angel. At that moment two escort ministering angels arrived and the individual was accompanied through the gate to their wonderful eternal destination on this NARROW beautiful lighted flowered tunnel. {**Praise God!**}

[Eternal life for this person not eternal death and suffering!]

{Matthew 7:13-14 … "Enter through the narrow gate. For wide is the gate and broad is the road that leads to destruction [Hell], and many enter through it. But small is the gate and narrow the road that leads to life [Heaven], only a few find it.

[Be Afraid, Be Very Afraid]

There is an order on how things are done in both heaven and the second heaven; this second-dimension realm order was Satan's. This place will be your final judgment. Hell is disorder; Satan is lord there. Make sure you are ready for the right road. You will never die, wherever you end up, remember the choice was yours! Paige was so scared she was fearfully awaiting her fate; while still looking around she could not understand why there were so many wells, they were everywhere. They looked like stone a type material grayish, black in color.

These wells resembled the same wells that were around in the years 1700-1800 AD when you drop the bucket down the well you brought up water. But there was no bucket, and no rope attached to it, just creepy stone wells and they were only a few feet high. Paige could not believe what she was seeing. There were many scattered naked people, she watched in horror as the grotesque, disgusting, foul, disfigured demon she hadn't seen yet, reached its long nails and scaly hand out of one of the wells.

This huge horrifying demon was carrying a chain. She heard the horrified screams of a young man standing in front of this beast. "Alex," Paige screams. It was her boyfriend while alive on earth; he looked and saw Paige briefly. They were both screaming to each other, as Paige watched in horror as the demon, which made Alex look so small, swung his chain at Alex. It looked like the thrashing of a bullwhip. The chain wrapped around Alex's knees and waist; he fell immediately on to his belly. Alex was screaming helplessly. The demon dragged Alex like a hunter with a small rabbit on a rope. Paige watched Alex disappear down into that dark hole, [**an opening into hell**]. Alex was **screaming**, **screaming** and **screaming** the whole way down; this cut through Paige.

{2 Peter 2:4 … cast them down to hell and delivered them into chains of darkness}

[Be Afraid, Be Very Afraid]

Alex as you now realize died at the scene of the accident, along with Paige. Alex actually died before Paige, now it is her turn; the demon is coming for her, from the depths of Hell. They come to meet you at your coming.

{Isaiah 14:9 … below is all astir to meet you at your coming}

[Be Afraid, Be Very Afraid]

Paige is beside herself there is nothing she can do, nothing. Paige looked behind her and yes, she was in front of an entrance into **hell**. She could hear movement in the well as she stood in front of it, like the scratching on a chalkboard; as much as she wanted to run, she was paralyzed and could go nowhere. As horrified as Paige was, she meant nothing to the order that was in this second heaven; business was still being conducted all around her. She saw many more demons going through the funnel to earth, to deceive people.

The three demons closest to her were pride, lust and unforgiveness they left on their mission. At that moment an angel of the Lord glided up to Paige and looked into her eyes. Paige saw her life flash before her through his radiant eyes. She witnessed her many sexual encounters, the love of everything wicked and the love of her crystal. There was no God in her life, Paige sadly knew this. It took only seconds for the angel to review her life; she witnessed the car crash with the group of friends she hung with. She saw herself die.

Paige looks at the breath-taking Angel, and pleads with him to help her. She's terrified and he knows this, his eyes are full of empathy and compassion for her, but there is nothing he can do. God is love; to walk with God is to not fear. Paige is at the place of judgment, and everlasting punishment is coming for her, she is terrified. Be ready for the Day of Judgment!

{1 John 4: 16-18… God is love. Whoever lives in love lives in God, and God in him. In this way, love is made complete among us so that we will have confidence on the Day of Judgment, because in this world we are like him. There is no fear in love. But perfect love drives out fear, because fear has to do with punishment. The one who fears is not made perfect in love.}

[Be Afraid, Be Very Afraid]

[God's wrath is righteous and just. Paige had many opportunities to know God and accept Jesus as God's Son, who died for our sins.]

{Romans 1:18 … the wrath of God is being revealed from heaven against all ungodliness.}

[Be Afraid, Be Very Afraid]

Paige looks back at the well and sees the claws of a demon reaching out slowly, to bring Paige to hell. Paige's arms reach for the guardian angel, but she cannot touch him, she continues to cry out, "Please no don't let it take me." The angel turns, and goes before another doomed naked person. The demon is now out of the well. We cannot imagine the terror Paige is undergoing, this demon smelled of a dead rotted stench. It had claws and slime all over it. It was fearfully enormous.

The foul disgusting demon was pleased to see little Paige; the fear in her gave him strength, and he walked right up to her and put his huge arm over her to let his foul slime drip down all over Paige's naked body. With his long black fingernail he touched Paige's soft white flesh [instantly the touch of his nail burned her flesh] and the demon grunted, "Enjoy, the fire is next." Paige was frantic the demon was messing with her and completely enjoyed terrifying her. There was nowhere to run nowhere she could go, this was hopeless.

Paige turned her back to the enormous demon and was able to crawl a few feet; she was trying so hard to get away. The demon allowed her to be at a perfect position for the chain. The chain was tossed around her knees and waist she was dragged on her belly like a rag doll; pulled down into the lifeless depths of hell. Paige was screaming out not to be dragged down that foul dark hole, she tried to hold on to the well, but could not! The demons at work all loved seeing another terrified lost soul being taken to their lord Satan.

DOOMED

Paige was being pulled down, down, and down into complete darkness never to see light again. The deepest of night with no stars cannot describe this. Her fingernails broke with every attempt to claw the ground not to be drug down the opening to **hell**.

The well walls seemed to be alive, the odor, screams and slime was all so disgusting. Paige could feel the living forms embedded in the walls moving all around her and crying out. Paige watched as the entrance to hell became smaller and smaller, as she descended deeper and deeper, it was closing in front of her very eyes. As her arms reached out for the last bit of light she continued to cry out until she could see it no more.

The closer she was to hell the hotter it was getting. Paige was frantic, she knew the center of the earth was hot with lava; she never imagined this was where hell is.

{Ezekiel 26:20 … I will bring you down with those who go down to the pit, I will make you dwell in the earth below, and those who go to the pit will not return.}

[Be Afraid, Be Very Afraid]

Smoke and soot began to fill the well; they soon would reach the bottom. Paige began gasping she could not get a breath; this was awful not even air to breathe down here. Paige thinks to herself what did I do with my life to end up here in this God forsaken place. Paige continues to tremble and cry, she can't scream like she wants to, there is very little air, its torture.

Paige never even thought of Alex, she was consumed with the horrors she was experiencing. When she hit the bottom, it was dirty chalky dirt, very dry. The heat was unbearable; Paige thought she was going to throw up because of the rotten smells. What Paige could hear both saddened and terrified her; she heard the screams and cries of tortured victims everywhere. She could taste the stench of hell.

[Paige could not get over the fact that all of her senses still worked so well.]

{Matthew 5:29 … your whole body will be thrown into hell}

[Be Afraid, Be Very Afraid]

The demon dragged Paige through Hell to a holding cell. Paige's flesh showed signs of being dragged and slung around. Poor Paige, she will lose her skin and flesh eventually in this doomed place. Paige felt like she was in a jail cell. The only light was the lake of fire she could see in the distance.

She is absolutely frantic and consumed with fear. Paige could see what looked like many people in the lake of burning lava, they were all moaning in agonizing pain, like slowly being boiled alive for all eternity.

Paige could hear something behind her in the same black cell, she hysterically slowly turned around, and it was so black and dark. The flicker of the lake of fire made her cell look like a strobe light. Paige saw in the corner another terrifying demon, and with each flicker it drew closer, closer and closer to Paige.

This indescribable, horrifying demon was right in her face, only to stick its long pointy tongue out and slowly lick Paige's cheek. Wherever this gross tongue touched on Paige's face, her skin would burn and fall off. The demon licked his lips and said, "Fresh meat." Paige was horror-struck; she could feel every bit of skin being removed from her face.

Everyone that comes to hell first goes to the holding cells. When Satan is ready for you he will send for you, and you will call him lord; sadly Satan chooses where you will spend eternity, in this dead place. At that moment another disfigured enormous demon opens the cell door and grabs Paige's arm. The other demon grabbed her other arm, you would think they were trying to purposely pull her apart but they were ordered to take her to Satan.

Their communications with each other would be in grunts. Where were they taking her, Paige wondered? She was absolutely frantic, shaking and trembling with fear. She saw many pits {Holes in the chalky dirt} and she heard moans from these pits. Paige was close enough to look down into one of the pits. "Oh God," Paige cries out!

This could not have been a person at one time she thought to herself. It was nothing more than a pitiful skeleton frame of a person whose very soul was still alive; this person was moving and moaning he was suffering so much. There were flames underneath him. There was very little flesh hanging on his bones. "Why isn't he dead," she cries out!

One of the demons looked at her and with a hideous smirk replies, "There is no God here and you will never die." Paige was doomed and she knew this, she had never thought of this while alive on earth, you die and become a ghost or you are reincarnated, this was her thinking. Paige realizes how deceived she was. There were so many pits, with so many cries, from so many people.

[The pit was big enough to sit in with lots of worms and fire.]

{Luke 16:24 … I am tormented in this flame}

[Be Afraid, Be Very Afraid]

{Psalms 88:6 … you have laid me in the lowest pit in the darkest depths.}

[Be Afraid, Be Very Afraid]

This place has no feelings, no love, no compassion just pure pain, suffering, and ultimate evil. Satan's thrown in Hell, is the dungeon of all horrors. The screams and moans of tortured humans are the loudest in this awful place. The demons were heading right towards it. Paige was to march in front of the king of terrors {Satan} to find out her final fate.

{Job 18:14 … and they march him before the king of terrors.}[Satan]

[Be Afraid, Be Very Afraid]

When the demons entered lord Satan's dungeon and drew closer to his throne, they threw Paige down in front of him. She fell on her knees with her head down; she was too frightened to look up at Satan. When she was brought into the room of horror, she could not believe what she saw. Paige assumed it couldn't get worse.

[Don't assume anything Paige, your wrong.]

What she saw was so terrible and repulsive. These were people that at one time had all their flesh and bones; they were no longer recognizable. Many doomed victims were hanging from chains by hooks, most of them had chunks of flesh taken from them, and others had very little flesh left on their burned charred bones. All of them still very alive, and feeling everything intensely. Paige witnessed a demon snatch a piece of meat from a poor souls, rib and eat it, she watched the poor soul shake uncontrollably and cry out because of this unbelievable torture, he also had worms feasting on his flesh.

[How awful to be slowly eaten alive and never remembered and never die]

{Job 24:20 ... the worm feasts on them; and you are no longer remembered}

[Be Afraid, Be Very Afraid]

There were many stone alters with people chained to them, all these victims were burned beyond any recognition. They were chained to these alters awaiting their fate; again, they will never die. Paige had also witnessed a demon cutting off a person's leg for a meal as she was brought through the dungeon. {**This place is Death!**}

That poor person felt every bit of flesh being torn from his leg, the demon's teeth smash together {**gnashing of teeth**} the person trembling because of the pain from the torture, Paige could not even tell if this person was male or female, this was all too horrible to take in.

{Matthew 24:51 ... and will cut him in to pieces... where there will be weeping and gnashing of teeth.}

[Be Afraid, Be Very Afraid]

While on her knees all Paige could see was Satan's feet and legs. When she barely raised her head, she saw his long sharp black fingernails coming out of his fingers and his grey dead leather like skin on his arms that laid comfortably on the stone armrests. It was so frightening to be looking at so much power and evil, and to know her forever fate was his decision. Paige was trembling she had not yet felt the suffering she knew was coming her way.

Satan was exactly what you would imagine him to look like. The disfigured toes, with darkish grey and black long toenails, the dead leathery grayish brown skin all over his cold heartless body; his strong arms and his hands had long, black, sharp, pointy fingernails, sand he sat on a huge stone like chair, this was Satan's throne. When before her eyes Satan began transforming from terrifying to Perfection. His feet, legs and hands were spotless, smooth and beautiful. And why not, Satan was at one time an angel of the Lords, a beautiful angel; he can still deceive God's children as the angel of light.

[Satan is the greatest fallen spirit. Remember he will try to deceive you with partial truths!!!]

Satan transformed again to horrific, and since Paige would not look up at Satan the demons yanked her to her feet. She was trembling uncontrollably. The fear she was feeling cannot be described. Satan's lifted his right hand and pointed with his long black fingernail. The demon knew what the next order from Satan was, and left to assist another demon entering the dungeon. Satan had a surprise for Paige. Another hopelessly lost person was brought in to parade in front of Satan and find out his fate.

It was poor Alex!

Satan lavished in the fact they died together, he got both of them at the same time, he would use this to add more fear which Satan loved and thrived on. He is and always will be the ultimate to bring pain and suffering to anyone. Paige and Alex looked at each other. "Alex," Paige fearfully cries out! The demon that escorted Alex from the holding cell took a huge bite out of Alex's shoulder and was actually still chewing when he stood in front of lord Satan. Satan again lifted his right hand a bolt of fire hit the chest of the disobedient demon. Satan was the only one to decide everyone's fate.

Remember eventually this will also be Satan's permanent resident. After Satan sees you, all disorder takes place; you will be game for anything in hell. Paige could not believe the flesh gone from Alex's shoulder. Satan saw the terror all over the two of them; this was complete pleasure for Satan; he was able to torture and do with them as he wished.

[Not like God's child Job that Satan had to ask permission from God to hurt him.]

{Job 2:4-7 … Satan replied, "A man will give all he has for his own life. But stretch out your hand and strike his flesh and bones and he will surely curse you to your face…" The Lord said to Satan, "Very well, then, he is in your hands; but you must spare his life." So Satan went out from the presence of the Lord and afflicted Job with pain…}

[Be Afraid, Be Very Afraid]

Satan will afflict a lot of pain and he does not have to answer to God, you now belong to him! God has no part of hell, His mercy remains in the Heavens.

{Psalm 36:5 … your love and mercy, O Lord, are in the heavens}

[Be Afraid, Be Very Afraid]

When Paige looked at Satan, he looked like he was on fire, but he did not burn, he just laughed. Alex who while on earth was popular, good-looking, with lots of money. Here he is broken, humbled and terrified. Satan blew from his breath at Alex, and fire consumed poor Alex.

The fire felt like acid. Alex was screaming so much, Paige was screaming for Alex. The demons held Alex firmly, while he was standing there burning for a while in front of their lord, after all they had eternity to enjoy afflicting pain and torture. Alex's hair burned off, his skin was on fire. Alex was screaming as hard as he possibly could. Paige is crying out and screaming for Alex. Even though the demons are holding Alex while he is on fire they are not affected by the flame. When Satan blew again towards Alex, the flames subsided.

Remember this is your forever body so everything will happen much slower. Alex looked like he had third degree burns all over his body. Again, Satan lifts his finger; the demons understood the next order. Alex was terrified and frantic and in severe pain with his raw skin and burned flesh completely covering his young naked body. This enormous beast yanked him to a stone altar, laid him down on it and chained him down. Alex at that moment was Hell's entertainment, inflicting torment and suffering is what they did. Satan and the demons thrive on torturing and inflicting suffering.

Alex was crying out for mercy, "Please stop hurting me, please I'm begging you!" Alex continued to shake uncontrollably because of the pain, as he cries for mercy. All the other poor tortured souls in Satan's dungeon were glad for the moment; they were not the center of attention. Again, another of Satan's silent but understood orders was given. Paige was horrified she was crying out on behalf of Alex,

"Please stop hurting him, please stop." The demon that was following the order returned with a large bucket of burning coals. He began at Alex's feet slowly pouring the burning coals on his already sensitive, tender raw flesh. Alex was shaking uncontrollably and screaming out, "Oh God please, oh God please let me die!"

[Satan is Alex's lord now and he will never die! The hot burning coals continue.]

{Psalm 140:10 ... let burning coals fall upon them; may they be thrown into the fire, into miry pits, never to rise.}

[Be Afraid, Be Very Afraid]

Paige frantically watched in complete horror, as the demon slowly kept pouring burning coals on Alex. Alex will never go into shock, or even pass out from the pain, not in this place. Alex's bald burned head looks over to Paige, his eyes revealing the absolute, intensified; unimaginable, suffering he was enduring. Satan was enjoying watching the terror, fear and suffering he was ordering; this was so refreshing to Satan. After all, this was new virgin meat to torture. The hot burning coals were now as high as Alex's waist, the demon continued to cover him with the fiery coals.

{Psalm 11:6 ... on the wicked he will rain fiery coals and burning sulfur...}

[Be Afraid, Be Very Afraid]

The coals were being placed on Alex's raw chest; Paige could not bear to hear him cry out any longer. She just could not stand it, he was suffering so much. Paige runs over to where Alex was chained and tries to let him know he is not alone, she is there with him; Paige reaches out to hold his shaking hand. The instant she touched his hand she was set on fire. [**Satan laughs!**]

There is no pleasant touch here, the only touch you will ever get, brings pain. Paige is screaming she is consumed by the fire. Paige falls on to the chalky black dirt screaming and rolling, trying to put out the fire that has covered her naked body.

{Jeremiah 4:4 ... my wrath will break out and burn like fire because of the evil you have done and burn so that no one can quench it.}

[Be Afraid, Be Very Afraid]

Both Alex and Paige scream out in pain for quite some time, after all it's not like Satan has anywhere pressing to be. New people enter into hell regularly. But for now, Paige and Alex are the new virgins here. What has felt like hours has only been a short period of time; Alex and Paige are laying there being burned alive.

[This everlasting destruction will never end!]

{2 Thessalonians 1:9 … these shall be punished with everlasting destruction.}

[Be Very Afraid, Be Very Afraid]

WHO'S NEXT?

Let's go back to the accident. You can see Paige and Alex's lifeless bodies being covered up and placed in the back of the ambulance. Devin and Jayden are still pinned in the crushed vehicle. The machine called the Jaws of Life was on its way to cut them out. They both were not moving. Lucky was lying on the ground getting some much-needed medical attention. Lucky's left hand getting partly cut off was not the problem. Lucky's ribs had broken badly and they cut right into his lungs.

They emergency medical team were doing the best they could until they could get Lucky to the hospital. The ambulance took off with Lucky barely alive and strapped in. There was so much damage to his lungs he just could not be saved. Lucky stopped breathing and died while on the way to the hospital.

Lucky has his eternal body now and in the heavenly realm awaiting his judgment.

{2 Peter 2:9 … and to hold the unrighteous for his day of judgment…}

[Be Afraid, Be Very Afraid]

[Note: When you go to be with the Lord forever your body will be perfect, another reward from our awesome daddy God. So if you were blind, you will now see all of the breath taking sights of heaven, if you were deaf, you will now hear the most beautiful noises ever imaginable and if you had any body parts missing, they will be restored for you. You will be completely whole and new.]

[Heaven is the complete opposite of hell!!!]

Lucky was laying there noticing his left hand was partly cut off. Lucky is also naked and cannot believe what he is witnessing.

{Ezekiel 32:25 … yet they bear their shame with those who go down to the pit.}

[Be Afraid, Be Very Afraid]

Lucky cannot believe all this is real. He sees the demons that are sent back to earth to deceive mankind. He witnessed envy, selfishness, jealousy; lust and depression leave together through one of the funnels. Lucky doesn't witness a man wearing a radiant garment and being protected by the guardian angels like Paige did. Only FEW really do make it to Heaven. No one is willing to deny himself and put others first. Do you truly understand and comprehend how very short your life is here on this earth, but the affects from being here chooses your eternal fate?

[Repeat this daily!!!]

[More of you God, less of me! Repeat, repeat and repeat! {John 3:30} It's not about me Lord! Repeat, repeat and repeat! Die to self.]

Lucky is only sixteen years old, what he will have to endure forever and ever is just unimaginable. Satan knows Lucky is coming home to be with him. Just like everyone is excited and awaiting your arrival in Heaven, everyone is excited and awaiting your fate in hell. Lucky sees the long frightening claws slowly coming out of the opening to hell. He is horrified and cannot move.

The demon is enormous and terrifying, the strongest of men are nothing compared to these hideous fallen angels. A chain is thrown and Lucky screams while being pulled down, down and down he is banished.

{Job 18:18 … He is driven from light into darkness and is banished from the world.}

[Be Afraid, Be Very Afraid]

When Lucky finally hits the bottom, the chain is now around his waist and he is able to walk. No holding cell for Lucky, the demon was ordered to bring him straight to Satan. The fire in hell is so intense; there is no air to speak of.

(If you turn on your oven and allow it to get as hot as it possibly can, open the door and put your face as close as you can, try to take in a breath of air.)

[You won't be able to pull away in hell.]

{Malachi 4:1 … "Surely the day is coming; it will burn like a furnace. All the arrogant and every evildoer will be stubble, and that day that is coming will set them on fire," says the Lord Almighty.}

[Be Afraid, Be Very Afraid]

The hideous, foul demon was leading Lucky to the dungeon of horror. The screams and cries of the tortured people could be heard throughout hell. Lucky saw the fire that swept continuously through hell. It would enter a cell; Lucky walked past one and saw a person on his knees, covered by fire and screaming out. Then part of the fire would creep momentarily out of the cell and enter the next cell.

{Luke 16:23 … I am tormented in this flame}

[Be Afraid, Be Very Afraid]

Other cells that Lucky passed, he could not see into them, it was so black the blackest of black; he clearly could hear the moans of pain and suffering from inside. A skeleton arm and hand covered in holes and worms reached out of a cell in front of Lucky.

The poor person was pleading for mercy and begging for a drop of water. The demon hit the pitiful, begging arm.

{Luke 16:24 … that I may dip the tip of my finger in water and cool my tongue for I am tormented in the flame.}

[Be Afraid, Be Very Afraid]

(When I say you have all your senses in hell, you do. That scripture in the Bible should make you aware of that fact, you have a body after death, your eternal body, with all your senses, only to add to extra excruciating, unimaginable pain and suffering.)

Lucky has tasted, smelled, seen and heard a glimpse of hell; he is drawing near to lord Satan's dungeon, now he will feel hell. The demons inside the dungeon are still torturing Alex and Paige. The demons lifted burned Alex off the stone altar; they toss him on to the dry chalky dirt next to Paige who is laying there curled up and burned. Alex and Paige are still suffering so much; the pain and suffering will never end, never.

When Lucky entered the dungeon, he was absolutely horror-struck and sickened by what he was witnessing. How could they still be alive, while he looked around at the people, hanging by chains with chunks of flesh missing from their bodies, or next to no flesh on them at all, they were all burned by fire. All the altars were foul and horrid with poor tormented rotting souls. Lucky is so scared, so very scared.

Why didn't he listen all those years when he went to church? His belief was you died and that was it. Lucky was wrong!!! Lucky wishes he would have listened and **REPENTED**, and walked right with God. It is {**Too Late**} for Lucky! The demons toss him down in front of Satan. Satan asks Lucky if he recognizes his friends. Lucky turns around slowly. He sees the two-burned individuals lying on the ground, they were crying out from pain in front of Lucky.

Both Alex and Paige heard Satan say Lucky's name and they both slowly looked up. "Oh my God, Paige, Alex is that you," Lucky questions? Paige was the sister Lucky never had. Paige was one of the reasons Lucky was here. Lucky could not believe his eyes; his friends were unrecognizable and had been tortured horribly. He felt so sorry for them!

{Psalm 32:10 … many sorrows shall be to the wicked.}

[Be Afraid, Be Very Afraid]

[No horror film out there could come close to the reality of hell.]

Satan was exhilarated in the fact he had all three of them together and he knew the rest would follow. The last two were Devin and Jayden; Satan wanted them real bad, both of them at one time had a relationship with his enemy God, especially Jayden! This would grieve God.

[Satan wanted nothing more than to hurt God. Satan wanted Jayden and Devin!]

[God loves us so much He sent His only Son Jesus Christ to go through a horrible death, because of our Lord Christ bloodshed, we can be forgiven and reconcile with God.]

{Romans 5:9-11 … since we have now been justified by his blood, how much more shall we be saved from God's wrath through him! For if, when we were God's enemies, we were reconciled to him through the death of his Son, how much more, having been reconciled, shall we be saved through his life! Not only is this so, but we also rejoice in God through our Lord Jesus Christ, through whom we have now received reconciliation.}

[Be Afraid, Be Very Afraid]

Lucky is beyond frantic at this point! Satan blew the scorching fire on to Lucky's whole body and enjoyed the music of intense pain coming from his screams.

{Psalm 11:6 … a scorching wind will be their lot.}

[Be Afraid, Be Very Afraid]

While Lucky was laying there screaming, Satan lifted his finger with its long dark nail. A demon yanked up Paige and took her to a small dark cell where worms, rats, locust, snakes and demons will all enjoy the fresh meat. The burning fire will never end. Alex was also dragged out of the dungeon then he was placed in a hole in the dirt called a pit. Alex will also not be alone. His flesh will either be eaten on, or he will be on fire day and night. There is no hope for them!

{Isaiah 38:18 … those who go down to the pit, cannot hope for your faithfulness}

[Be Afraid, Be Very Afraid]

There is no hope for Alex, Paige or Lucky. It is {**Too Late**} for them!

Satan has not placed Lucky yet. Even though the fire has subsided from Lucky's body for the moment, he is absolutely petrified. Satan has decided to throw Lucky into the lake of fire. The lake of fire removes flesh quicker, no need to waste perfectly good meat. Satan gives the order and one of the poor souls that had been hanging there the longest, with no flesh left on his bones, was taken down to be tossed into the forever burning lake of fire. They then hung poor Lucky by chains with hooks, he was screaming out, "Please no, please no!"

A demon beast took his sharp claws and ripped open Lucky's rib cage and devoured it. Poor Lucky he is only sixteen years old, he will live forever in this absolute horrible indescribable place.

[God warns us, we will be destroyed like this if we are against him! Fear God!]

{Hosea 13:8-9 … I will attack them and tear open their rib cage; I will devour them and tear them apart. You are destroyed because you are against me}

[Be Afraid, Be Very Afraid]

{Hebrews 10:30 … "The Lord will judge his people. It is a dreadful thing to fall into the hands of the living God."} **[Be Afraid, Be Very Afraid]**

Chapter 6
OUT OF GRACE

*B*ack to the accident on earth; Devin and Jayden are being taken out of the crushed car. The entire top part of the car had to be cut off just to get them out. Jayden was semi-conscious and moaning in pain. There was blood coming out of her mouth because of her massive internal injuries. Devin's head hit the window knocking him out; his arms remained protectively wrapped around Jayden the whole time. The kids were rushed to the nearest Hospital. Jayden had serious internal injuries; the ambulance called ahead to inform the hospital that there was an emergency situation. On call surgeons were awaiting the arrival of the kids.

[Satan and hell were also awaiting the arrival of the kids!]

{Romans 6:23 … For the wages of sin is death, but the gift of God is eternal life in Christ Jesus our Lord}

[Be Afraid, Be Very Afraid]

When Jayden and Devin were brought into the hospital the emergency team of doctors began evaluating the damage. Jayden was going to have to go right into surgery, there was internal bleeding they needed to find and stop. Devin was still unconscious; he was taken to get a CAT scan, MRI and X-rays, they detected his shoulder had been broken. The concern for both kids was substantial; they were both in critical condition. The police had retrieved the kid's licenses from the accident scene and were on the way to their parent's homes to inform them of the tragedy involving their children. By this time, it was early in the morning.

When the police arrived at Alex's home they had to knock for a while before his dad finally answered the door, his mom was still asleep from drinking too much on New Years. The Police had to do the toughest part of their job and that was to inform a parent that their child was killed in an accident and they needed to identify the body. This was too much for Alex's dad to handle, he gave his son everything and he loved him dearly. This was his only son, tears filled his eyes.

[Fathers love your child by training them to know God and be terrified of not knowing Him.]

{Ephesians 6:4 … Father bring your children up in the discipline and instruction of the Lord.}

[Be Afraid, Be Very Afraid]

{Deuteronomy 6:6-7 … These commandments that I give you today shall be on your heart; day and night diligently impress them on your children.}

[Be Afraid, Be Very Afraid]

Alex's dad woke his hung over wife and informed her about the tragedy of their son, that he was killed in an accident and their beloved son was no more. The screams and cries from Alex's mom woke the neighbors, this was the worst news a parent could get. Her son was the only reason she remained married to his father; she was able to continue with life because of the successful son she was raising. The officers had a female officer with them to assist in comforting Alex's mom. The father was too distraught to drive himself, so he rode with the officers to identify his dead lifeless son who he loved and spoiled so much in life.

[He would be really horrified if he could see what was happening to his son at this very moment. Poor Alex the worms have covered him and he is being slowly eaten and he is continually on fire, this is unbelievable pain and torture he will endure throughout all of eternity. Alex's dad will be able to identify Alex's body on earth, but he could not possibly be able to identify his son right now and Alex just got to his new forever home, a horrific pit in hell. Alex is not dead, he is very much alive, what they have already done to him in hell is unimaginable.]

[If Alex's parents understood the seriousness about a personal relationship with God and instilled this in their son they loved so much, and themselves, they would have enjoyed eternity in an awesome place together forever and ever called heaven.]

{Psalm 139:8 ... If I go up to the heavens, you are there.}

[Be Afraid, Be Very Afraid]

Alex's dad was on his way to identify his son's body. At this time the police were at Jayden's house informing her parents Jayden was in an accident and has been taken to the Hospital. They quickly got dressed and rushed to the hospital to find out how their daughter was doing. When the officers arrived at Holly's house, Paige's mom and Lucky's foster mom was sitting on a swing on her front porch.

Holly performed psychic readings for an income and she was not able to sleep because of uneasiness in her spirit she had been feeling. Paige was Holly's world, she cared for Lucky but Paige was her daughter, her only child.

When the officers told Holly both her daughter and Lucky had been killed in an accident, she went to her knees and cried out hysterically. The officers had to calm her down before asking her to come and identify the bodies. Holly was devastated and her baby girl was no more. What Holly does not realize, is if she continues this life style and does not repent and become saved through the blood of Jesus Christ our Savior, Satan will bring Paige to the dungeon when Holly arrives in hell. Holly will see the horror of what her daughter looks like.

[Satan loves to have entire families in hell!]

When Holly sees hardly any flesh on her precious daughter, just a burned, pitiful, skeleton framed, tortured captive, this is the worst possible thing a parent will ever have to witness, but it will be {**Too Late**} for Holly at that moment, like it is {**Too Late**} for Paige her daughter and Lucky.

God loves us so much He gave His only Son to be sacrificed for our sins. Believe, ask, and spend eternity with God and your loved ones.

[Here life on earth is so short with family, but heaven is forever!]

{1 John 4:9-10 … This is how God showed his love among us: He sent His one and only Son into the world that we might live through Him. This is love; not that we loved God, but that He loved us and sent His Son as an atoning sacrifice for our sins.}

[Be Afraid, Be Very Afraid]

The officers are taking Holly to identify both Paige and Lucky's bodies. When the police car arrived at Devin's house, no one was home. Devin's parents and sister were spending the weekend at the Cocoa Beach Hilton. Keri, Diane's best friend was walking her dog when she saw the officers pulling out of the driveway. She explained she was a good friend of the family and they were away for the weekend.

The officer told Keri, Devin was in a bad accident and is in Cape Canaveral Hospital. The officers went into Keri's house and called the hotel. The front desk put them through to their room. They were sleeping, Diane answered the phone and the officers gave her the news. The officers got done talking and looked at Keri and told her Devin's parents were on their way to the hospital. Keri thanked them and said she also was going to the hospital to support her friend.

At this time Jayden's parents arrived at the hospital to find out Jayden was being prepared for emergency surgery. They needed the parent's consent form signed. Jayden was still bleeding internally and not doing well. James, Diane and Bella arrived at the hospital; Keri arrived right behind them. Devin was still being evaluated on all the damage done to his body. While Jayden was being rushed into surgery she stopped breathing; her parents sadly witnessed this and cried out to God, "No God please, don't take Jayden!"

[It won't be God that takes this beautiful young girl!]

The emergency doctors worked on reviving Jayden for fifteen more minutes, but Jayden could not be revived; she is dead. Jayden's earthly body is dead; now she has her forever body and she is very much alive. Jayden is sitting in the second heaven terrified and awaiting her judgment.

{Ephesians 1:20 … he raised him from the dead and seated him in the heavenly realms.}

[Be Afraid, Be Very Afraid]

JAYDEN

Jayden could not believe she had died and that this was really happening. She saw hideous demons everywhere. Four of these grotesque demons approached Jayden before exiting through a funnel to earth. These demons were anger, rebellion, lies and hardened heart, they wickedly laughed at Jayden and said, "We deceived you and you will be turned over to lord Satan, he anxiously awaits your arrival." This horrified Jayden and she cried out, "No that's not true, I know who God is, I believe in Jesus!" "I asked Jesus into my heart when I was eight years old, she screamed out!" They continued to circle her and terrify her. Jayden kept crying out that her Lord was Jesus!

{Matthew 7:21 … not everyone who says to me, 'Lord, Lord, will enter the kingdom of heaven, but only he who does the will of my Father who is in heaven.}

[Be Afraid, Be Very Afraid]

The demons continued to hiss, tease and terrify Jayden. These demons knew her very well; they were the ones that worked so hard to get her away from God's grace and fellowship. While Jayden laid there naked, she noticed one person who was wearing a long flowing garment and standing in front of a beautifully lit flowered pathway to heaven.

Jayden then witnessed a huge, disfigured demon dragging a man by a chain to hell, she was absolutely terrified. She heard him screaming as he was dragged all the way down that black well. All of a sudden Jayden looked up and saw a powerful light.

Everyone at work in this dreaded doomed place of judgment suddenly stopped what they were doing as their attention was drawn to the intensifying bright Heavenly light.

Out of Heaven itself Jesus descends down to the realm of judgment. Jayden watched as Jesus approached closer and closer. All the demons fearfully backed away from Lord Jesus, the angels stood at attention, Christ the Lord was in their presence. Jesus' eyes were full of tears; he loved Jayden so very much. "Jesus," Jayden cries out!

Jesus was radiant full of light and power; He was magnificent to look upon. Tears began rolling down his cheeks. Jayden saw her life on earth through His heart felt eyes. She saw how she had stopped having fellowship with God and stayed angry at her parents. She was consumed with lies and rebellion, her heart had become hardened. She saw the accident and her death.

[She saw she had not REPENTED; she was not pure and Holy!]

{Hebrews 12:14-15 … without holiness you will not see God, see to it that no one misses the grace of God.}

[Be Afraid, Be Very Afraid]

All of a sudden, an enormous and very strong demon reached out of the well behind Jayden. His long claws alone terrified her. "Please Jesus don't let this demon monster take me, Jayden profoundly begs." The demon hisses at Jesus but is terrified and stays back. "Jayden, I love you so much, God the father did not spare the angels that sinned, He cannot be a part of any sin, God My Father is just," Jesus said grievingly.

{2 Peter 2:4 … For if God did not spare angels when they sinned, but sent them to hell, putting them into gloomy dungeons to be held for judgment.}

[Be Afraid, Be Very Afraid]

{2 Timothy 4:1 ... In the presence of God and of Christ Jesus who will judge the living and the dead...}

[Be Afraid, Be Very Afraid]

The demon fearfully hissed again at Jesus. Jayden was Satan's and he was thrilled to get another one of God's precious children, to do with them as he wished. Jesus, tearfully left Jayden and slowly ascended into heaven.

[Jayden will be forgotten, remembered no more.]

{Psalm 6:5 ... For in death there is no remembrance of you.}

[Be Afraid, Be Very Afraid]

The enormous, foul, chilling demon threw Jayden to the ground; he wrapped the chains around her beautiful body and legs. Her hands tried to claw in the ground to resist, but the amazingly strong demon dragged her screaming and terrified down the black well to hell.

{Luke 9:42 ... the demon through him to the ground...}

[Be Afraid, Be Very Afraid]

This was absolutely horrifying beyond belief; Jayden will never see light again. Jayden has known hell was real for a while, she never believed she would ever end up there. Satan has worked on tricking Jayden for years. It began when she was not allowed to go with her friends to a Christian retreat called Acquire the Fire. This angered her; she felt she was right and her parents weren't acting Christ-like. The more her parent's judged people and praised themselves because they believed they were perfect Christians, the more Jayden wanted nothing to do with their religion or their God. The saying that her mom said all the time went right through Jayden.

Faults in others I can see, praise the Lord there's none in me.

{Matthew 7:3 … why do you look at the speck of sawdust in your brother's eye and pay no attention to the plank in your own eye?}

[Be Afraid, Be Very Afraid]

Satan is the master of deception and will use whatever means he can to get you away from fellowship and a personal meaningful relationship with God. Jayden's heart was beating so fast, she is scared to death of small areas. Going down, down and down she was frantic beyond belief. The smell was nauseating and revolting, there was movement in this descending black hole. Jayden knows the Bible and she knows she will be here for all eternity. She is horrified, completely hysterical while descending down.

{Proverbs 7:27 … is the way to hell, descending to the chambers of death.}

[Be Afraid, Be Very Afraid]

Jayden is only seventeen years old, what she has to endure throughout eternity, is inconceivable and unimaginable.

Satan has ordered Jayden to be taken straight to his dungeon of horror. Satan has wanted Jayden badly since she was eight and turned her life over to Jesus. Satan was angered that Jayden was the reason other kids got saved. One of the kids that got saved at her house, will actually be the reason many kids turn their lives over to Jesus Christ; he becomes a powerful youth pastor. She proudly always invited her friends to her house during church service. Satan is going to make her pay dearly for that.

[Smoke was coming from the bottom.]

{Revelation 9:2 … smoke rose from it like the smoke from a gigantic furnace}

[Be Afraid, Be Very Afraid]

They have reached the bottom; this is beyond horrifying, the rotted stench of human flesh all around her, and the cries from tortured victims, the unbearable heat and lack of oxygen. Jayden is so horrified; it is black, black and black beyond belief. Nothing absolutely nothing is worse than hell!!!

[Satan lost the battle in Heaven and his only drive is to HURT GOD! Satan wants to lead God's children astray].

{Revelation 12:7-9 … And there was a war in heaven. Michael and his angels fought against the dragon, [Satan] and the dragon [Satan] and his angels fought back. But he was not strong enough, and they lost their place in heaven. The great dragon [Satan] was hurled down-that ancient serpent called the devil, or Satan who leads the whole world astray. He was hurled to earth, and the fallen angels with him.}

[Be Afraid, Be Very Afraid]

The chain is around precious Jayden's waist and arms as she is being taken to Satan's dungeon of horrors. Jayden is Satan's now; for the moment she is still such a beautiful girl. [**Not for long**]! Jayden is so absolutely horrified; her heart could not race any faster as this absolutely grotesque and foul demon pulls her to the dungeon of horror! To think at one time she enjoyed the beautiful ocean and sunshine, she was full of life. Only now to be full of death; Jayden is being taken to be slaughtered.

[This place is a tomb, a furnace in the earth and Jayden will never see light again, for all eternity.]

{Psalm 49:19 … they shall never see light}

[Be Afraid, Be Very Afraid]

Jayden is trembling all over from fear. Ahead she sees lit torches. She hears horrible screams from so many unfortunate people that would go through anyone. As she is taken closer, she sees many horrifying demons sitting on stone benches and wickedly enjoying disgusting entertainment.

This was their arena to enjoy watching the dismemberment of poor hopelessly lost individuals. The more the demons cheered, the more torture was going to be inflicted on that person in the center of the arena. Everyone that goes to hell will have their turn in the arena. This was the place the demons enjoyed playing twisted games. Jayden watched as she slowly walked around this brutal place.

A gigantic demon just ripped off the arm of this poor person and hid it from him. This unlucky person screams were horrendous, as he was set on fire, he had to find his ripped off arm that had been hidden from him. He had to play or suffer more broken off limbs.

{1 Samuel 2:10 … those who oppose the Lord will be broken in pieces.}

[Be Afraid, Be Very Afraid]

Jayden had never witnessed such pure evil and gruesome activity. The demons hissed at her, they wanted to be the first to tear her white soft flesh from her bones; everyone knew lord Satan is first with hell virgins! Jayden could feel these enormous sickening demons hated her in a horrible way.

They were dreadful angry fallen angels, the ones who lost the war in Heaven along with Satan. Satan's death chamber is just up ahead. Jayden hears more horrifying screams from within. She is so very terrified. The demon gladly tosses Jayden down in front of Satan. "Who is your God now Jayden, Satan questions?"

Jayden is so horrified she knows she is forever lost with no hope. She saw absolute terror when she entered this chamber of death. The poor chained up hanging victims, all suffering so very much and all very alive. Jayden hears her name called from behind her. She looks back and sees a person burned beyond recognition, with chunks of bone and flesh gone from him. He was hanging from hooks with chains.

Again, a tormented voice says, "Jayden." A demon with sharp teeth and long pointed fingernails headed towards this poor lost hanging soul.

As Satan hideously laughs, he asked Jayden why she did not recognize her friend Lucky. That poor tortured victim calling out to Jayden was Lucky. The demon touched Lucky with his long fingernail and Lucky was set on fire again. The demon laughed, he wanted his meat well done. At that moment a huge foul snake wrapped around Jayden as if to smother her. Jayden was a Barbie doll to this monstrous snake.

{Deuteronomy 32:24 … I will send against them the fangs of wild beast and the venom of snakes that glide in the dust.}

[Be Afraid, Be Very Afraid]

Jayden's worst fear was confinement. Jayden was pleading for mercy from lord Satan. Satan was going to make Jayden suffer greatly. Satan lifted his hideous fingernail and Jayden began to feel her tender flesh burn up with that unquenchable fire. She was completely covered by fire; this fire did not affect the foul massive snake that was wrapped around her. She could not breathe and was suffering so much.

[Lucky was shaking uncontrollably from the continued torture.]

{Matthew 13:50 ... you will be thrown into the fiery furnace, where there will be weeping and gnashing of teeth.}

[Be Afraid, Be Very Afraid]

{Revelation 9:6 ... men will seek death, but will not find it; they will long to die, but death will elude them.}

[Be Afraid, Be Very Afraid]

DEVIN

Meanwhile back at the hospital where Devin fights to live. Devin's collarbone was broken; there were also two additional breaks to his right arm. The hospital placed a body cast on Devin all the way up to his shoulder. The concussion he suffered was also a concern. His internal organs had been crushed and he would have to remain in the intensive care unit for observation. The next forty-eight hours were critical. Satan knew Devin was on his way to hell and he would be there very soon.

Satan was preparing Jayden for their reunion. Devin will not recognize Jayden his first love; he will not be able to recognize poor Lucky either. Devin's mom Diane had found out everyone else died. She had just had all the kids over for Christmas a week ago. Diane was frantic, she could lose her son and she knew he was not spiritually ready.

Life is so short, those poor kid's families Diane thought.

[We can't predict when we will die; we need to make sure we are ready.]

{Psalm 78:39 … a passing breeze that does not return.}

[Be Afraid, Be Very Afraid]

Devin was in his room now and Diane is at his side. She is holding her son's hand and praying to God. James her husband comes into the room and Diane lashed out at him, "You have never cared for Devin; don't act like your concerned now." Tearfully she continues, "Take Bella home, I'm not leaving my son." James knows those harsh words from Diane were the truth, and he felt awful, he had always been unloving to Devin. James left with Bella and informed his distraught wife everything would be taken care of, she was not to worry about anything, and to remain with her son. Keri came in to the hospital room; she wanted to support her friend Diane.

Diane is crying to her friend as she holds her son's hand, "He's not ready Keri, he can't die, please pray he makes it through this, and he is not ready to die. I have to know he is going to be with Jesus, he's not ready!" Keri hugged Diane to comfort her. Keri informed Diane that she left a message at their church about the accident. It was Saturday now and Diane and Keri have stayed beside Devin, he has still not woken up.

Keri left momentarily to get coffee for Diane and herself. When she returned the Pastor and his wife entered with her. They were recently informed about the horrible accident and they wanted to let Diane know they were there for her and her son. She was so grateful, the four of them laid hands on Devin and the Pastor began praying for him.

[The prayer was intense and hopeful and in this room of despair you could feel the awesome presence of the Lord.]

{Matthew 19:13 … were brought to place his hands on them and pray for them.}

[Be Afraid, Be Very Afraid]

The wonderful Pastor and his precious wife gave hope and encouragement to much needed Diane. They informed her Devin would be prayed for in the morning by the whole church. Diane was so grateful, she believes in the power of prayer.

Satan is hopeful Devin won't make it through the night; Satan has Jayden looking unrecognizably perfect for Devin's arrival in hell. How very sad! Devin loved Jayden so very much. It is early evening now and Diane remains at her dearly loved son's side. Keri has also remained there the entire day with Diane. Devin begins to moan and Diane grabs his hand and says, "Devin its ok, mom is right here, you're going to be alright." Devin opens his eyes and frantically looks at his mom.

Death is coming for Devin. "Mom it is so dark, don't leave me, I'm afraid," Devin cries out! He continues, "don't leave me Mom it's so dark so very dark!"

[God tells us we will be raised for judgment!]

Devin stops breathing, his heart stops and is no more.

{Psalm 55:4 … the terrors of death have fallen upon me.}

[Be Afraid, Be Very Afraid]

{1 Corinthians 6:14 … By his power God raised Christ the Lord from the dead, and He will raise us also.}

[Be Afraid, Be Very Afraid]

Diane watched her son take his last breath of air and die. Diane is hysterical, she screams out, "No God please, no don't let them take my baby, God please, God please, oh God please don't let them take my baby!" The emergency team came in to revive Devin. They tell Diane to leave the room; Keri and Diane exit the room.

Diane immediately falls to her knees and cries out to God so loud that hospital staff come running. Keri puts her hand out to the staff to stop and let Diane cry out to God that her son's eternal fate, which is destruction and death, be saved.

{Daniel 6:10 … he got down on his knees and prayed.}

[Be Afraid, Be Very Afraid]

Devin was at the place of judgment, he is terrified. Terror is all around him in this dreaded place, he is doomed and he knows it.

{Psalm 73:19 … suddenly they are destroyed, completely swept away by terrors!}

[Be Afraid, Be Very Afraid]

Devin laid there frantic, he is a whole person, he feels, thinks, smells, hears and yes, he sees, his entire senses feel magnified. Devin sees the demons everywhere, he watches an enormous foul demon come out of the opening to hell and drag a woman screaming back down the hole. Devin is devastated.

[You have your whole body alive when you are taken to hell!]

{Psalm 55:15 … let them go down alive to [hell] the grave.}

[Be Afraid, Be Very Afraid]

Devin wished he would have listened to his mother's pleas to get his life right with God. He has always believed there was life after death, but he didn't want to give up any of his precious time to God. There was always going to be in his busy life something going on, or somewhere to go, or someone to see.

[God makes time for you, make time for Him!]

While Devin was looking around, he did not see any robed persons going to Heaven, all he was witnessing was the ones going to hell. There were many!

[That is why it says Eternal Life or Eternal Death. Going to hell is your Second Death.]

{Revelation 21:8 … their place will be in the fiery lake of burning sulfur. This is the second death."

[Be Afraid, Be Very Afraid]

Devin is so scared he can't move; he is nothing more than paralyzed prey waiting to be picked up by the hunter and taken to be helplessly slaughtered. Gigantic claws slowly creep out of the well behind Devin. Satan has a welcome home present for Devin, his precious Jayden awaits Devin's arrival in hell; Satan wants Devin to see the flesh and hair gone from her and to witness her horrible fate. This foul huge demon with his long scary claws, grabs Devin's right arm, the touch of the demon burned into his flesh. Devin cries out in horror and pain he feels everything.

All of a sudden, a magnificent awesome light shines down from Heaven. It was as if the Heavens were opening up. The demon was watching the light from Heaven and could not leave with Devin; this angered the evil devouring demon.

Diane, Devin's mom was crying out to God completely whole heartily and would not stop her cries for her son. These intense, loud cries, went through the hospital, and have reached Heaven, and have reached God!

[They were the true cries from a mother [who is a child of God] trying to save her child, from despair.]

God knows this heartbreaking cry; He cries daily, for His precious children, that He loses to Satan. All of a sudden, a legion of angels descends from Heaven, armed and ready for battle. The second heaven realized this was happening, and also stood for battle. You could not even count all the angels and demons that were face-to-face, awaiting God's command for battle. These grotesque demons were facing majestic angels of the Lord Most High. Devin was surrounded by good and evil; the foul demon releases Devin's arm leaving burn marks in his flesh, he will always have these scars.

Jesus brilliantly and magnificently descends to the place of judgment; there is a battle going on over Devin's soul. The demon hissed at Jesus but remained fearful, "He is Satan's you know this, he is not yours!" Jesus protectively reached for Devin as soon as he did, it thundered and lightening. God has spoken, the demons were trembling, but angry, and they knew Satan wanted Devin. God has heard the powerful heartfelt tears and cries from his precious child Diane, Devin's mother. Mothers' tears saved her son! Diane is right with God!

{Proverbs 15:29 … The Lord is far from the wicked but He hears the prayer of the righteous.}

[Be Afraid, Be Very Afraid]

Jesus' warm and wonderful loving eyes looked into Devin's eyes and silently express to Devin, you will not have another chance, do right with your life and save souls from this eternal fate. Your mother's cries have been heard throughout Heaven!

[Jesus has warned Devin of this coming wrath.]

{Matthew 3:7 … warned you to flee from the coming wrath.}

[Be Afraid, Be Very Afraid]

 Jesus continues to inform Devin to go back to his body on earth. How marvelous, to be in the presence of Christ the Lord! Devin is vacuumed back like he was when he was brought to that place. Devin was back in his room at the hospital, he could hear his mother's heart wrenching cries for him, and Devin slips back into his lifeless body. The hospital staff was successful in reviving Devin. A nurse rushes out to inform Diane of the good news and to calm her down. When Diane runs quickly to her son's side, you still saw overwhelming tears all over her face.

 Devin looked refreshed, alert, and happy to see his beloved mother. "Mom God heard your prayers, you saved me,"

 Devin says softly to his mother. Diane just threw her motherly arms around her beloved son and she continued to weep, she thanked God for hearing her cries!

[Devin has escaped hell!] [You may not!]

{Matthew 23:33 … How will you escape being condemned to hell?}

[Be Afraid, Be Very Afraid]

Devin's whole life changed because of this horrific experience. He has dedicated the remainder of his life here on earth, to service and youth. His relationship with his mom and stepfather has completely healed. He has become a big part of his Church. It has been twenty-two years since he died, and Devin remembers the ordeal like it was yesterday.

Devin has become the youth Pastor of his church. It is a beautiful Sunday morning; he will be leaving soon with his wife and daughter to attend church. Devin is sitting on his desk with his Bible open holding a picture of himself, his dear friends and his beloved Jayden; none of them returned to earth. Devin is the second boy from the right in the aged photo. His left hand holds the photo as his right hand gently touches each one of these kids.

As he touches each one, he smiles and has memories of a special time they had together, while alive on earth. Devin's eyes begin to fill with tears; he doesn't believe they escaped hell, like he did. As the right hand [this is the same arm that the demon from hell left burn marks in his flesh] touches each kid, Devin wonders where they have been for the last twenty- two years.

Still Alive

Devin's focus on the picture of all the kids is of Lucky first. He smiles remembering; Lucky at the beach bringing everyone pizza he had stolen. Devin remembers the first hurricane that hit; Devin and Lucky remained up talking while everyone else was asleep. He remembers Lucky's wacky Halloween costume and when his mother gave Lucky a Bible. He had become close to Lucky and Devin wonders where his dear friend is, what he is enduring. After many years of unbelievable torment and suffering in Satan's dungeon; Lucky was taken and thrown into the lake of lava and burning fire. Lucky is there with many other hopelessly lost souls.

All are clenching their teeth together in forever pain, unmerciful suffering and pitifully crying out.

{Matthew 25:30 … thrown into the darkness, where there will be weeping and gnashing of teeth.}

[Be Afraid, Be Very Afraid]

Lucky has not yet been taken to the arena of dismemberment where the dreadful demons add extra torture to victims for their unimaginable gruesome games. He is still missing part of his left hand, this is the only way we know it is Devin's sixteen year old friend Lucky. He is trying to crawl out of the unbearable burning lava, that he has lived in for many years. He feels it all, even though Lucky has no flesh left on his young bones, he still feels excruciating pain.

Demons watch everyone in the burning lake of fire and no one is allowed to escape, they are to always be suffering. Lucky crawls out of the fire hoping for a second of relief. He is completely nothing more than a burned skeleton; his soul is alive inside his skeleton frame. This is too sad to understand. The foul evil demon swoops down and yanks Lucky up like a boy grabbing a small doll, and the enormous beast tosses poor unfortunate Lucky back in the Lake of fire.

[These demons are his executioners!]

{Job 33:22 … His soul draws near to the pit and his life to the executioners of death.}

[Be Afraid, Be Very Afraid]

Devin still remembering his friends looks at Alex in the picture now. Alex was so handsome and had it all. Devin remembers how well Alex surfed. Devin smiles thinking of all the Hurricane parties that were at Alex's. He remembered how they always received special privileges at the football games because of Alex. The time Alex opened up personally to Devin about his family situation. Devin wonders where his dear friend has been for the past twenty-two years. Alex is still in one of the many pits in hell, he is pitiful to look at.

His flesh has wasted away; you see his bones sticking out everywhere.

{Job 33:21 … His flesh wastes away to nothing, and his bones, once hidden, now stick out.}

[Be Afraid, Be Very Afraid]

Alex has not been taken to the horrifying arena, but he will go soon. When he is not on fire, he is being eaten on by worms. His eyes and nose are just holes. He is completely covered by worms and they continually eat at him, it feels like scorpions. They hurt so badly! His bones are full of holes!

{Revelation 9:5 … And the agony they suffered was like the sting of a scorpion when it strikes a man.}

[Be Afraid, Be Very Afraid]

He is so very thirsty. Because of constantly being set on fire he only has soot to breathe in. Alex cannot get a breath of any refreshing clean oxygen. Every part of him is in agonizing pain. There will never be rest for Alex! He will burn alive forever!

{Mark 9:48 … thrown into hell where their worm does not die and the fire is not quenched}

[Be Afraid, Be Very Afraid]

Alex will be in forever pain and suffering for all of eternity. He will be with Satan and his demons forever and ever, and at such a young age, how absolutely horrifying. Devin is now touching Paige's picture on the photo. Paige always complimented how well Devin treated Jayden. Devin remembers how Paige and Lucky would act like brother and sister and how much Paige loved her mother Holly and Paige was Jayden's best friend. Where has Paige been Devin wonders deeply, what has happened to her? Paige has lived for the last twenty-two years in a dungeon cell. Her forever home is the size of a small table that seats four people. Like Alex, she also has been tormented by the flesh-eating worms and the unquenchable fire.

To Paige's misfortune, the demons are leading her to the arena. Anyone in the cells goes to the arena more often; they are unfortunately the closest to that God forsaken place. You cannot recognize Paige. She fits right in with all the others who forgot God, while alive on earth. While in the arena at this very moment, Paige screams out in unbelievable pain, an unfeeling demon just tore off the bottom of Paige's right arm.

This was hidden from her and again she is set on fire and has to find her ripped off lower arm or suffer greatly!

{Psalm 50:22 … Consider this, you who forget God, I will tear you to pieces, with none to rescue.}

[Be Afraid, Be Very Afraid]

Holly, Paige's mom has just passed away from a heart attack. She never repented, or acknowledged God the Father or asked for salvation through Jesus Christ the Son. The arena games on Paige will thankfully have to be cut short. Satan has ordered Paige be brought to him. He wants to grant Holly his devoted servant, with her witchcraft and psychic readings, her dream while she was alive on earth.

{Deuteronomy 18:10-13 … Let no one among you practice or engage in witchcraft, or cast spells, or who is medium or spiritist or who consults the dead. Anyone who does these things is detestable to the Lord. The Lord God will drive you out. You must be blameless before the Lord your God.}

[Be Afraid, Be Very Afraid]

All Holly ever thought about while alive on earth, was the wish to see her beautiful daughter, one last time alive! Holly's daughter Paige is very alive, and Holly is about to get her wish. Again, Satan loves entire families in hell! Paige was brought in first she is terrified her arm aches where it was ripped off. What will Satan inflict upon her now? She has suffered so greatly these many years. [**Twenty-two years is nothing compared to eternity!**]

Paige is thrown to the ground; her pitiful body is almost all skeleton form with some hanging flesh left on her, her soul lives inside her burned charred bones. She will remain alive forever!" I have a surprise for you Paige," Satan wickedly says. Paige had not been here since she first was brought to Satan. She wondered if Satan was going to bring Alex back in front of her. Paige sees her mother Holly and cries out, "No please not her."

Holly is terrified, she sees death and torture all around her, only no one was dead. "Holly, don't you recognize your daughter, she's alive, I'm granting you your wish to see her one last time," Satan cruelly says with a hideous laugh. Pitiful Paige looks up and with very little strength cries out, "Mom." Holly is frantic consumed with fear, she was the reason they were both here; she was so deceived and misguided.

Holly desperately reaches for Paige. "No mom don't touch me," Paige cries out! {**Too Late**} as soon as Holly touched Paige, they were both consumed with the unquenchable fire!

{Deuteronomy 32:22 … for a fire has been kindled by my wrath, one that burns to the realm of death below.}

TOO LATE

[Be Afraid, Be Very Afraid]

Devin is still looking at the photo; the hardest one for him to think about was his first love Jayden. Devin always tried to protect Jayden when they dated, he could not protect her wherever she has been living. Devin takes his finger and he gently rubs her picture. He remembers how hard he tried to find out her name. He remembers their first date, and their first kiss at the beach. The way they slow danced, and lost their virginity to each other.

Devin's eyes are watering, where has his beloved Jayden been, what was her eternal fate? Satan took it out on Jayden, when he did not get to bring Devin to eternal damnation. Satan's enemy God let him go. Jayden knew God at one time, this even made it worse on her.

[There is no hope for Jayden; she can never praise God again!]

{Isaiah 38:18 … For the grave cannot sing your praise; those who go down to the pit cannot hope for your faithfulness.}

[Be Afraid, Be Very Afraid]

Jesus gave his last goodbye to precious Jayden; all of Heaven will never remember she ever existed. God has said this, so it will be. Poor Jayden, she will be forgotten and never found!

{Ezekiel 26:21 … "I will bring you to a horrible place and you will be no more. You will never again be found," declares the Sovereign Lord.}

[Be Afraid, Be Very Afraid]

Jayden had a fear of small areas; she still remains in a coffin. This is the blackest darkest place in hell.

{2 Peter 2:17 … Blackest darkness is reserved for them.}

[Be Afraid, Be Very Afraid]

    She cannot move even an inch and when Jayden was thrown into this horrible place, it was full of worms to constantly give that scorpion sting on her already raw flesh; they will never stop eating at her flesh and she will never die. She is always on fire; the demons make sure of this. The demons keep turning her coffin of death like their roasting a pig.

{Isaiah 66:24 … their worm will not die, nor will their fire be quenched…}

[Be Afraid, Be Very Afraid]

    Jayden is given extra torment to her unimaginable suffering. The foul demons were ordered to constantly jab her coffin with spears. Each time they do, you hear worn out Jayden's whimpering or groaning from more insufferable pain and torture.

{Too Late} for Jayden!

{Psalm 6:6 … I am worn out from groaning.}

[Be Afraid, Be Very Afraid]

    Devin has tears running down his face, as he focuses on Jayden. Devin is now married; his wife and four-year-old daughter come into his office. She sees the tears, and the picture he is holding, and knows what he has been thinking about. His wife walks over to aide in support, and puts her arms around her husband. She lovingly says, honey we need to get going, we don't want to be late for church; your parents are meeting us there."

She then looks at their beautiful four-year-old daughter and says to her, "Jayden go get your Bible, mommy and daddy are ready to leave." Devin gives his precious daughter a strong, heart-felt hug before she leaves the room. Devin places the picture back in his used Bible, wipes his eyes again, hugs his wife and heads to church.

Devin is going to help bring as many people as he can, into the **Kingdom of Heaven and wake them up to the truth about forgotten hell and Satan! FEAR GOD!!!**

Please Read Important Scriptures

{Deuteronomy 18:13 … You must be blameless before the Lord your God!!!}
[Be Afraid, Be Very Afraid]

{Luke 13:3 … I tell you, unless you repent, you too will perish.}
[Be Afraid, Be Very Afraid]

*{Matthew 4:17 … "**Repent**, for the kingdom of heaven is near."}*
[Be Afraid, Be Very Afraid]

{Matthew 10:28 … Don't be afraid of those who want to kill your body; they cannot touch your soul. Fear only God, who can destroy both soul and body in hell!}
[Be Afraid, Be Very Afraid]

{Romans 10:9 … That if you confess with your mouth, "Jesus is Lord," and believe in your heart God raised Christ from the dead, you will be saved.}
[Be Afraid, Be Very Afraid]

{John 3:36 … Whoever believes in the Son has eternal life, but whoever rejects the Son will not see life, for God's wrath remains on him.}
[Be Afraid, Be Very Afraid]

{Ephesians 6:17 … Finally, be strong in the Lord and in His mighty power. Put on the full armor of God so that you can take your stand against the devil's schemes.}
[Be Afraid, Be Very Afraid]

MY DECISION TO RECEIVE CHRIST AS MY SAVIOUR

Confessing to God that I am a sinner, and believing that the Lord Jesus Christ died for my sins on the cross and was raised for my justification, I do now receive and confess Him as my personal Saviour.

The End!

May God Be With You!

About the Author

I am a faithful, committed and loving wife, mother and grandmother. Really, I am a-nobody to the world's standards, I love to serve, and for a living I humbly clean houses. But God had plans for me, like He does all of us. I would rather let others tell about me.

My Beloved Husband

Hello! I'm Mark Lund, Denise's husband. I've truly been blessed by God to have such a wonderful God-Fearing wife. She loves God with all her heart and it shows. She has studied the Bible since she was a young girl; I love when she preaches to me and tells me about different scriptures and stories in the Bible. When God came all over her to write this book *"Too Late"*, God also came all over me to help her in any way that I could to make this book a reality and get it out into the world to help Save Souls. It truly changed my life when I read it. Everything written in *"Too Late"* is real, and she has the scriptures and passages right there to back up the story she wrote. I love you Denise, you are {Proverbs 31:26… she speaks with wisdom, and faithful instruction is on her tongue.}

Love your husband,
Mark Lund

My Wonderful Son Dane

I am the youngest child; I can honestly say I am truly blessed to have been raised by my mother, Denise Wright Lund! We never had a lot of money but I never lacked for anything. Spoiled I was not. Mom taught me at a young age her responsibility was to take care of my needs, and I was to take care of my wants. She is the hardest working woman I have ever met. Difficult times have come our way, my dad Mark could not work due to an accident and he required many surgeries. Mom never complained, she has incredible faith in God. One of my needs was Spiritual Growth; mom made it a number one priority that I know who God the Father, Jesus the Son and the Holy Spirit was! You did not want to be disobedient, not with the way my mom prays. Trust me, God hears her prayers. I look back now and realize there was always someone who had no family, at our family events, or someone with a broken heart calling mom for prayer, or the doors being opened for the homeless to find shelter and warmth. Mom taught me we are not here for ourselves but for others. I read this powerful book. It is from God. It was life changing for me. I love you mom and it's not *{Too Late}* for me, we'll spend eternity in an awesome place together, thank-you mom for your continued prayers!

Love your son,
Dane Lovell

My Precious Daughter Tiah

Being a mother myself now has made me realize the incredible, powerful servant of God my mother is. I was raised in church and thank-you mom for that. Mom taught me there is power in prayer and that God is there for His children. A man was angry and should not have been driving, Mom laid her hands on the dash board of the van and prayed out loud, "I can't stop him Lord but you can, in Jesus' name," she said; the dash board immediately caught on fire. Many times, I had friends in serious trouble and I always called my mom for prayer. I understood the presence of God early in my life, thanks to my mother. When people shunned the lowly or poor, mom taught me the opposite and as a teenager at one time in my life, with the van that poppy Mark and mom bought me, I loaded it up with unsaved teenagers and brought all of them to a revival called Acquire the Fire; they all got saved. Knowing God was very important while I grew up, and I was a missionary at a young age. My mom and I have always had a very special bond, I will always love and appreciate her, she is so much more to me than just a mother; she now has become my best-friend! I'm proud of you mom and I know you are obeying God.

Love your daughter,
Tiah Casher

My Spirit Filled Sister Michelle

To my dear friend (my twin) Denise… I am forever grateful to you for sharing your book *"Too Late"* with me. I have known **OF** you since high school but never got to **KNOW** you until our 25th high school reunion. For some reason we were drawn to each other and have now been the best of friends for 7 years. I'm starting to understand, after reading your book, why God brought us together at that reunion and not earlier in life. His plan for us together is a powerful one and I believe it has **saved** my life! I **was** somewhat of a lost soul and wasn't sure what I was supposed to do or what I was supposed to believe… Now I know… And for me it won't be "**Too Late**" thanks to you. I pray I can reach out to people through your book and they too will find their way. I love you with all my heart, you are a true friend! I am totally blown away and amazed as I watch you reach out to so many people, some that you don't even know. I will always love you and be there for you… see you in heaven.

Your eternal friend,
Michelle Hoskins

Bibliography

Book
New American standard Bible
Zondervan

_____
_____
_____
_____
_____
_____
_____
_____
_____
_____
_____
_____

Work our your own Salvation with Fear and Trembling. Philippians 2:12